Praise for The Adventures of Charlie and Moon

"*The Adventures of Charlie & Moon* is a maniacally funny book that takes you inside the vivid imagination of Martin Meader where we meet a wacky cast of characters that we come to love and join in a wild adventure told with unbridled humor and language so rich you will ask yourself how someone could have thought of it! Children will love the non-stop action and disgusting hilarity, adults will marvel at the mind of this writer, reminding them of Roald Dahl in all his wicked glory. I love this book!"

Jana Laiz, Award Winning Author of
Weeping Under This Same Moon

"*The Adventures of Charlie & Moon* is charming! It will appeal to a wide range of children but should be especially welcome to younger fans of the Harry Potter books. It has the classic feel and lovely language of Tolkien but with plenty of contemporary bits. I particularly liked the wonderfully flowery descriptions of people and places. The 'English-ness' might have turned off some readers before Harry Potter but now even the youngest kids know what 'cream buns' and 'waistcoats' are. I also love that the violence is kept low key & somewhat cartoon-y. I can't wait to have it in the store."

Kat Goddard
New England Children's Booksellers
Advisory Council Member

The Adventures of Charlie & Moon is an eccentrically hilarious piece of work. I loved every page. Totally enjoyable for all ages!

Zoë, age 16, USA/Philippines

Published by Crow Flies Press

Copyright© 2009 by Martin Meader
ISBN 978-0-9814910-1-1

Library of Congress Control Number 2009936013

Visit us on the Web! www.crowfliespress.com

Printed in the United States

Cover art work by Dawn Meader
www.dawnmeader.com
Cover design by Adam Rothberg
www.adamrothberg.com

Mixed Sources
Product group from well-managed
forests and other controlled sources
www.fsc.org Cert no. SW-COC-002283
© 1996 Forest Stewardship Council
FSC

The Adventures of Charlie & Moon

Book One

Facing the Quincequonces

By

MARTIN MEADER

Dedication

This book is dedicated to the memory of my mum and dad,
Joe and Joan,
my brothers Graham and Russell, my sister Kathryn
and my fantastic son,
Charlie-Moon.

Acknowledgements

ed•it•or [ed-i-ter]—noun. A person who edits material for publication, films, etc. I've often wondered what an editor actually does but after having worked with the gifted Jana Laiz (the editor of *The Adventures of Charlie & Moon*), I now know. Editors move you to a new level. They challenge you, make you laugh, almost make you cry and show you there is more. Much more! I am indebted to Jana and her incredible commitment. Working with her across the Internet (between Perth, Western Australia and Egremont, Massachusetts, USA) has been a wonderful experience. We have two more books to write in this trilogy and I can't wait to begin!

A special mention must be made to Irena Mihova, my good friend and fellow producer who followed the dream without ever doubting that this book would happen! And to Deb Saville and Lindsay Breach for their unending support and passion.

To all the other people who have helped and inspired me along the way, I offer my deepest thanks and gratitude. They are:

Lauralee Alben, Ann-Elizabeth Barnes, Zufan Bazzano, Colin Beasely, Jane Belotti, Marie Bowen, Kosta Cami, Julia Chazan, Rod Christian, Suzanne Coy, Maeve Dillon, Nick & Sindhu Dobree, Bram Fisher, Nellie Flannery, Sheila Francisco, Jeff Fusco, Emily Graham, Kat Goddard, Gerald & Sandra Groom, Robert Hachey, Suzanne Harper, Luke Haskell, Mark Higham, Pauline Howell, Van Ikin, Tracey Kaplan, Len & Lena King, Harold Klemp, Rachel Konowitch, Zoë Laiz, Chanel Marriot, Jojo McDonald, Teresa McClelland, Charlie-Moon Meader, Dawn Meader, Graham and Jacqueline Meader, Russell and Nikki Meader, Ashley Meczywor, Wilbert Molenaar, Dacre Montgomery, Caitlin Partridge, Donna Peerce, John Prossor, Bree Renz, Paul Riegelhuth, Brian & Gwen Saville, Kencana Shinta, Jarad Spence, Rob Spence, Rylie Spence, Caroline Van Tilborg, Freya Tingley, Debra Ann Townes, Gwen Tunnicliffe, Jennyfer Vallejo, Diana Wallace, Thomas Williams, Kevin Yeung, Ashleigh Zinco.

Prologue: A Seed Is Sown

It was an unusually warm night in the shire of Tumblegum. The long, winding, dirt track that led from the two-story, ramshackle farmhouse on top of the hill seemed to lie in waiting. The happy babble of motorbike frogs and clackety crickets filled the star-lit landscape. Christmas was only five days away and the land felt as content as it ever had. So, when a large bank of clouds innocently meandered towards the moon, no one took any notice. Well, not until the moon disappeared completely. Then a cold chill invaded the darkness and everything came to a stop, stood absolutely still. Even the frogs and crickets became silent: frozen in mid-croak, as it were. There was a sudden air of expectancy, as if something strange was about to happen. Then something strange *did* happen.

Stepping across into the hot Tumblegum evening from an otherworldly blizzard, a peculiar-looking gentleman stood on the farm's porch dusting the snowflakes off his heavy greatcoat. Steam rose from his woolen scarf. His sturdy black boots stretched up above his knees and he carried a gnarled, wooden walking stick. Taking off his gloves, he reached deep inside his coat pocket and pulled out a small, shiny golden package.

Waiting on the verandah in the shadows of the night were Cecil and Sylvia Ramsbottom, the owners of the farm. They had been expecting the old gentleman, though they were more than a little shocked to see remnants of snowflakes on his coat, melting in the hot summer night. The man looked at the couple and smiled sadly. Then as if weighing his decision carefully, he passed the golden parcel to Sylvia, gently touching her arm in reassurance.

As one, Cecil and Sylvia spoke, "We will give it to him. You have our word." The traveler replied, "Thank you and good luck. One day he will understand." Turning to leave, the man stopped, his head tilted to one side, as if listening to an unseen voice. Reaching yet deeper into his greatcoat pocket, he pulled out a second, larger parcel, wrapped in shiny silver paper. He handed this to Cecil, who received it graciously, their eyes locking for a long moment. "He will need this too!" said the man. Nodding his head in understanding, Cecil bowed to the old visitor whose smile was now hopeful. The old gentleman turned and made his way down through the blooming garden, breathing deeply the roses that scented the gravel track leading to a very creaky bus shelter. The couple watched him go, gave each other a knowing look and went back inside the farmhouse.

Once the man reached the bus stop, he sat down and drew in another deep breath of the warm air, filling his lungs with the sweet smell of mother earth. Slowly expelling the air from his weary frame, he glanced uneasily back to the farmhouse and tugged worriedly on the long white beard that grew out of his face like a snowstorm of cottonwool.

Through the quiet of the night came the deep rumble of a large vehicle approaching. The man's ears shot up like a dog. Preceded by the gleam from its very bright headlights, a bus sped around the corner into view. It was the No. 9 and right on time. As the bus drew closer, lively South American music could be heard pouring from its windows. Inside the bus, a woman was performing the most rhythmic rumba dance. The moment she saw the man, the woman stopped dancing and, as she did, the bus screeched to a halt in front of him.

Now, if you had looked closely at the bus, you would have noticed the strangest thing: there wasn't a driver. Even more peculiar was the dancing ticket collector. Her name was Doreen Tremblingknees and from head to toe she was dressed in green. Doreen sported an enormous beehive hairdo that towered four hands into the air above her head and was surrounded by little honeybees, all trying to snuggle in for a cozy night's rest. Plumping her notorious hairstyle back into shape and away from her elfish ears after her wild dance, Doreen pushed a lever down at the back of the bus and the door hissed open. Gazing fiercely at the bearded gentleman, she finished chewing on a piece of honeycomb and gave a long squeal.

"Bizz-Buzz, there you are!" she called excitedly. "Is it done?" Bizz-Buzz twitched his ears but said nothing for the moment. Then he slowly looked at her, his enormous watery blue eyes betraying his feelings as he spoke. "What will be, will be, Dor-r-reen," he said, rolling his rrrs in a very gentle way. "It is my

3

business to do my best, and that is all one can do in this buzzed-up situation. It is our only chance and it now rests with the boy." Bizz-Buzz shrugged his shoulders and made his way to a seat inside the bus.

"The boy! Is he strong enough? Isn't he too young?" cried Doreen Tremblingknees as she followed him down the bus.

"He bore witness, Doreen. He bore witness. And, it is the king's will," said Bizz-Buzz making himself comfortable in one of the seats. "What's been bizzed cannot be buzzed. There's nothing more we can do but hope and t-r-rust."

Doreen rang the bell and started swaying her body slowly up and down the aisle. This was the signal for the bus, still without any sign of a driver, to crawl away into the darkness. Through the windows, Doreen could be seen moving her arms like the wind as she danced. And as she did, she sang a haunting medieval lament that wafted through the air:

The time has come for us to depart
I dance this bus with my broken heart
And put my trust in a spirit unknown
The gift has been given,
A seed has been sown.

For a while, it sounded as if the whole valley was crying, the song was so sad. But then, the bus rounded the corner and disappeared out of sight, silence falling upon the landscape once again.

Well, almost.

A small feathery creature had been hiding in some bushes

near the road, watching the proceedings. Panting and puffing, it dragged itself out from behind its cover. Checking backwards and forwards to make sure that no one was following, it stumbled along the pathway accompanied by an irritating clunking noise coming from a large piece of ugly, rusted chain that was attached to its bloodied right claw. Engraved on one link of the chain, were the initials, **S.W**. with the body of a rattlesnake wound around them. The animal stopped for a moment, touched a claw against one of its wings and then continued towards its goal—the ramshackle farmhouse on top of the hill.

Part One: The Call to Adventure

Chapter One: The Gift

Upstairs in the farmhouse, Mrs. Sylvia Ramsbottom was putting the children to bed. It was getting late as Sylvia said goodnight to her daughter Penelope. Thirteen-year-old Penelope was what you might call unusual. With a frenzy of red hair, she had an outlandish love of opera and horror movies. She reveled in singing along with famous operatic arias on her iPod. It was said that she had a voice that could strip paint off doors and at this very moment was badly singing *The Queen of the Night* from Mozart's *Magic Flute*. Penelope's other joy in life was numbers and on this night she was, as usual, furiously working at a laptop computer surrounded by a large assortment of math books cleverly stacked, pyramid-style on the floor next to her desk.

Sylvia Ramsbottom said goodnight and closed the door to her daughter's bedroom and headed across the landing towards another door. When she opened this door and peeked inside, it appeared at first sight, as if a tornado had ripped through the room. The room was chaos in motion. The walls were covered with posters of winged dinosaurs and snowboard heroes in mid-flight. Sylvia stepped delicately across the toy-strewn floor. Avoiding scattered bunches of Lego pieces, she made her way to a bed piled high with blankets. Stopping next to a very untidy bedside table, she called out softly.

"Charlie, where are you?"

"Under here, where it's warm and snugly," said a muffled voice that seemed to come from anywhere but the bed. Sylvia Ramsbottom slowly pulled the covers back to reveal a pile of pillows and a beautiful long skateboard inscribed with the word: LUCKY. Without warning, Charlie flew from his perch on the chest of drawers out in front of his mother. He screeched at the top of his voice. Sylvia pretended to jump back in fright—she'd been through this before. Charlie laughed out aloud and so did his mum. He stowed his skateboard under the bed with a clunk and climbed under the covers. His curly, blond head resembled a raggedy mop as it stuck out of his blue and white-striped pajamas. Turning onto his side, Charlie looked up at his mother who had on a weatherproof parka that she always wore around the windswept house. She had the same kind of moppy hair as her son. In fact, the two of them were probably cast from the same mop!

"Well, were you scared?" Charlie asked, as he picked up his clunky EM9 portable game-player and continued maneuvering a bird-like creature over an invented landscape.

"Of course," said Sylvia leaning her head to one side and smiling at her son. Taking a colored pencil from her parka, she reached up to the endangered species calendar above Charlie's bed. The month of December showed a bald eagle hovering over a city landscape. Sylvia drew a large blue circle around Friday the twenty-first and straightened a crooked framed newspaper article next to the calendar. The article showed a photo of the Ramsbottom family and two very large chickens with the headline reading:

RAMSBOTTOMS SAVE THUNDER EGG CHICKENS FROM EXTINCTION

"You know, Charlie," she said with a twinkle in her eye. "Tomorrow's a very special day but I can't remember why." Charlie continued to play his game, one eye glancing up at his mother.

"For one thing," said Sylvia playfully. "I know it's either the longest or shortest day of the year, depending on which side of the world you live on."

"Mu-u-u-um...give me a break, would you?" moaned Charlie navigating his winged creation over a mountain. Sylvia continued,

"That means that we've only got...let me see now...five more days until...well, would you believe it!"

"Would you be quiet in there?" Penelope sang out operatically from her bedroom. "Some of us are trying to compute in our sleep."

Charlie rolled his eyes. "Does she really have to be my sister?"

Sylvia Ramsbottom nodded her head gently and smiled to

herself. Taking a deep breath, she finished her sentence.

"...and, it's the last day of school tomorrow," she whispered, pretending excitement. "I can't think of any other reason for it to be a special day. Can you, Charlie?"

Still engrossed in his game, Charlie said, "It's my birthday tomorrow. You know it is."

"Oh, so it is. Well Charlie, this dreamer almost forgot...this," said Sylvia. She put her hand inside her parka and rustled some paper. Charlie sat bolt upright and placed the EM9 on the bedside table.

"You'll have to close your eyes first," said Sylvia. Charlie quickly put his hands across his face and tried to peek out from behind his fingers but his mother knew him too well. She waited patiently. So Charlie complied by squeezing his eyes tightly shut. From deep inside her coat, Sylvia carefully pulled out the small rectangular package. She held it in her hands in front of Charlie's face.

"You can open your eyes now."

The package, which was encased in gold wrapping paper, was so shiny that Charlie could see his warped reflection staring back at him like an ugly gargoyle. Sylvia placed the gift very carefully on the night table, next to his game-player.

"Charlie," she said. "This is from a friend called Bizz-Buzz." Charlie squinted, unconcerned with the identity of the giver.

"Bizz-Buzz! Fizz-Fuzz! Who cares? I want to open it now! Is it the latest version EM9?" said Charlie with all the patience of a hound dog on the scent.

Sylvia rolled her eyes and continued. "Bizz-Buzz gave me strict instructions that it should not be opened until morning.

So—promise? Do I have your word?" Charlie could hardly contain himself.

"Cross my heart and hope to…fly?" Charlie mumbled rather cheekily, giving an emphatic nod and raising and flapping his arms above his head. Mrs. Ramsbottom beamed at her son and kissed him on the forehead, leaving two shiny red lipstick marks just above the bridge of his nose. She made her way back across the room and turned around to take one more loving (almost knowing) look at her son.

"Sweet dreams, darling." Then she switched off the light and closed the door.

Ϲ Ϲ Ϲ Ϲ

Outside on the wooden verandah that encircled the farmhouse, the multi-colored lights of a Christmas tree gleamed and flickered in the quiet of the night. A *clinkety-clunk* could be heard down by the gate leading to the house. The small, feathery creature that had finally reached its destination was looking up at a large wooden sign, with an image of four people and two very large chickens, which read:

THUNDER EGG FARM
HOME OF THE THUNDER EGG CHICKEN
OWNERS: CECIL & SYLVIA RAMSBOTTOM

At that moment, the moon cleared from behind the clouds and lit up the entire valley. The front door to the farmhouse swung open and Charlie's father, Mr. Cecil Ramsbottom, resplendent in a tartan dressing gown with matching socks and sheep's-wool boots, wandered onto the porch to put out the milk bottles. The fluffy animal quickly dropped down behind a large bush of purple eggplants. Mr. Ramsbottom completed his nightly ritual, went back inside the farmhouse and closed the door. When all was quiet again, the downy creature switched its gaze to an upstairs bedroom where the lights had recently been turned off–the bedroom that belonged to none other than Charlie Ramsbottom.

☾ ☾ ☾ ☾

Snuggled under his blankets, the light from the EM9 illuminating the package, Charlie stared at the gift with bated breath. What was he to do? Should he open it or shouldn't he? He was a boy of his word...sometimes. He decided he would resist that particular temptation, at least for the next few minutes and reluctantly returned to his electronic adventure. Opposite his bed was a huge, double-door, oaken closet. As if a breeze was blowing through the room, the closet doors creaked open like they do in scary movies and the moon's silvery light revealed that Charlie's shirts and trousers were rocking backwards and forwards on their clothes hangers. His eyes darted to the window but it was closed. Scared, Charlie tried to keep his eyes fixed on the game. He gulped, or tried to but his mouth was as dry as a monkey's armpit. He could feel his heart thumping against his chest. Eerie shadows danced across the bedroom wall. He grabbed a bottle of water and was about to put it to his lips when a voice called to him.

"*Pick it up. Go on, pick it up,*" the voice urged hypnotically. With his hair virtually standing on end, Charlie's head spun around. The voice seemed to come from the package.

"*Pick it up. Go on, you can do it,*" called the charmer's voice. It was definitely coming from the package.

Very slowly, Charlie put his EM9 aside, reached out and put his trembling hands around the gold paper gift and felt it. He held it to his nose and smelled it. He shook it. He even tried to listen to it.

"Cross my heart and hope to...fly? Cross my heart and hope to..." The half-hearted promise that Charlie had made to his mother echoed around in his head. Quickly, he slid the package back onto the table and sighed. Why did he have to wait until morning? It was ridiculous and inconsiderate to leave a present by a boy's bed on the night before his ninth birthday.

"*Open it. Don't be weak. Be strong. Come on, open it.*" The voice drew him in again, so much so that he couldn't stand it any longer. Taking a deep breath, Charlie got out of bed and, putting his ear to the floor, listened for *Talk with the Animals*, the TV program that his parents were undoubtedly watching in the living room below. He knew they would be there for hours feasting on poached Thunder Eggs, completely engrossed. He crept slowly to the door, pulled it open very carefully and slid across the landing to Penelope's room. Peeking through the keyhole, Charlie could see Penelope, half hidden by algebra books and multiplication tables. Her computer was still aglow with a screensaver of her favorite scary movies. She was talking to herself, stretched out across her bed, fast asleep.

"Twenty-seven multiplied by nine equals two hundred and forty three..." mumbled Penelope. Now she was even being clever in her dreams. "What a waste of space," whispered Charlie to himself and stole back into his room.

With the coast clear, he turned on his bedside lamp and picked up the gift. Very carefully, he peeled back the sticky tape and meticulously undid the golden wrapping to reveal a book! On closer inspection, he saw that it wasn't even a whole book. It was half a book. He couldn't believe it!

"Half a book—what am I supposed to do with half a book?" Charlie grumbled.

The book's cover was encrusted with jeweled edges and a thin, silken band of blue cloth joined by a waxen seal held the book's remaining pages together.

Just as he was about to disgustedly place the book back into its wrapping paper, a silver sparkle danced off the waxen seal. Charlie took a closer look. The seal sparkled again. Now this was a different story!

Placing his fingers around the seal, Charlie tried to break the waxen padlock but it wouldn't budge. He tried again: still no luck. Then, he summoned up all the strength he could muster and with both hands, finally cracked the seal in two. As it snapped, so did the power in the house. Instantly, all the lights went out.

Absolute darkness!

Frantically, Charlie felt for his EM9 and tried to turn it on but its power had also been mysteriously drained. He then reached into the drawer of his bedside table. His fingers scrabbled about searching for something. Where was it? Ah, there, his flashlight. He turned it on, grabbed the gift, and dived underneath the bedclothes.

Gripping the flashlight with his teeth, Charlie examined

the cover of the book but couldn't see any kind of title. Then letters began to magically appear on the surface of the book:

..e ..ok .. .r...s

Then more letters.

.he .ook .r.ams

Followed by more.

.he .ook of .reams

As all the letters finally apppeared on the cover, Charlie read out loud, *"The Book of Dreams?"*

Another voice, a kinder voice, then called to Charlie, *"Weren't you asked not to open the present?"*

Charlie gasped and the flashlight fell out of his mouth. Picking it up, he shone the light across the book. On the cover, the title started to disappear. The book shook violently in Charlie's hands and the original title was replaced by slimy green letters, which read:

The Book of Skunk Weavel Rules!

A foul smell came from the words, making Charlie gag. Encircled by a long, red rattlesnake, they seemed to glow and writhe like worms. And if there were two things in life that Charlie hated, it was snakes and worms.

The first mesmerizing voice then hissed, *"You're not frightened of snakies, are you, little boy?"*

"Of course not," replied a terrified Charlie, adding indignantly, "and I'm not little."

Charlie quickly turned to the first page. There was a cartoon on the page that showed an ugly mouth with a flaky whiskery moustache. Suddenly, a long tongue shot out from the mouth and licked the lips, startling Charlie. The mouth formed a smile, displaying an awful set of dingy, crooked teeth. From the rank lips, words began to whisper; words that were slowly appearing on the page Charlie was staring at.

Welcome, my brave friend.
Bring this half of the book to me
and I promise life will never
ever be the same again.

Charlie turned to the next page. The mouth cackled a horrible laugh and disappeared only to be replaced by a very faint drawing of a feather and the much kinder voice that issued the following warning:

Charlie, you've broken your word
so you're in the story until you
finish it. Beginning right now!

Then the voice started to tell the story in the book...

The little creature kissed his mother
and father a tearful goodbye.
Silently sliding through a hole in
the dusty floor of the toymaker's workshop,
he began a long and tiring journey.

**Arriving at a farmhouse
after many days toil,
he climbed up to a bedroom window and
began to tap.**

Tap, tap, tap!

Charlie froze under his covers.

Tap, tap, tap. There it was again. He could hear his heart thumping against his chest.

Tap, tap, tap.

He definitely wasn't dreaming.

And he wasn't imagining either.

Someone or something was definitely tapping at the window.

Chapter Two: The Chosen One

Charlie was so terrified by the tapping at his window that his eyes glazed over and he fell into a trance, drifting deeper and deeper. Something very unusual was happening. The package: the package. He had opened it although he had promised his mother he wouldn't. He had broken his word. He had only wanted to have a peek and then he was going to put it back. Honest. But his word was no longer impeccable.

Charlie turned off his flashlight and listened again, hiding under the covers like a thief in the dark.

Tap, tap, tap.

Yes. There was most definitely something tapping at the window.

Carefully re-wrapping the book under the bedcovers, Charlie poked his head out of the sheets and nervously called out, "Hold on! Would you, hold on."

Tap, tap, tap...again! He lifted the covers off his head. The tapping was continuous and getting louder by the minute.

Quietly placing the package back onto the bedside table, Charlie curled his fingers around the edge of the blankets then ripped them off the bed. In the darkness, he began to blindly run towards the bedroom door. With his feet ooching and ouching from treading on the minefield of Lego and tin soldiers that littered the floor, Charlie tripped and fell against the door. Lying there, he heard a squeaky voice calling to him from outside the window.

"Let me in, let me in! I've traveled 10,000 eagle hops! It's important! Let me in! Pleeaasse let me in!" Charlie crawled towards the window. Raising himself up, he pressed his face against the glass, which began to steam up all around him. The high-pitched voice called out again.

"Pleeeaasse let me in! C'mon! I have an extremely urgent message for Mr. Charlie Ramsbottom!"

"That's me," said Charlie quite surprised. "Message, what message? Extremely urgent! Who's it from?"

"Listen-to-the-Wind," squeaked the voice, "Listen-to-the-Wind!"

Charlie was a very curious boy, but up until now, not an especially brave one. Tonight was different though. Tomorrow, he would be nine. He felt the blood rush to his head and with shaking hands, slowly unlatched the window. Gathering his courage, he pushed the shutter open as hard as he could. Somewhere out in the near-then-far darkness, there was a scream followed by a muddy thud. Charlie stuck his head out of the window and peered down into the garden below.

"Be careful!" squawked the voice. "You could have killed me." In the blackness of the night, Charlie could see nothing.

But he could hear something, a something that was slowly clawing its way up the trellis to his bedroom window. Before he could turn on his flashlight, he was standing eye-to-eye with a creature he had never seen before in real life; a young, proud eagle, one and a half hands tall with a large furry head and feet much too big for its body. Jutting out from the eagle's skinny frame were the first signs of a magnificent pair of blue and gold wings. Charlie stared at the young bird, as it stood panting and puffing on the window-ledge. Although he had only seen eagles in books before, there was an uncertainty, a question mark about this fledgling eagle. Instead of a hooked and pointy beak, he had a sort of friendly and straight...mmmm...what you might call...nose.

"Are you Charlie Ramsbottom?" enquired the eagle, looking slightly battered and muddy. Charlie nodded, his mouth wide open. He had heard parrots speak before but this was unbelievable. This bird was actually conversing like a person and Charlie could understand him!

"Prove it. Prove to me that you are in fact Mr. Charlie Ramsbottom," demanded the feathered intruder, peering right into Charlie's face.

"Prove it? What do you mean?" said Charlie, still taken aback.

"I have strict instructions. I can't go talking to any old Ramsbottom," said the eagle. Charlie thought for a moment and then ducked down out of the bird's sight.

"Here," he said, popping up again, pulling his library card out of his school bag. "This is mine." Charlie turned on his flashlight. The eagle grabbed the card and read it out loud.

While the bird was actually reading the card, Charlie noticed the branches on the huge mango tree outside his window move towards them as if to leaves drop on the conversation.

"Charlie F. Ramsbottom. Thunder Egg Farm. Mmmm, I suppose that'll have to do." Charlie examined the bird and saw the initials S.W. and a rattlesnake on the chain attached to the eagle's bloodstained claw. Something about the initials bothered him, but he couldn't figure out what it was.

"Wakey, wakey," said the bird, diverting Charlie's attention. "Are you going to let me in so I can give you the message?"

"Not until I know your name and who sent you," repeated Charlie, shaking a little.

"Just let me in. We haven't got much time!"

"But who sent you?" insisted Charlie, plucking up his courage. "Who sent you?"

"Listen-To-The-Wind," cried the exasperated eagle, "Listen-To-The-Wind."

"I don't understand. What do you mean, listen to the wind?"

"Are you going to let me in or aren't you?"

"Only if you tell me your name and who sent you."

The branches of the mango tree jumped back a little as the bird turned and gave a worried look up into the night sky.

"My name is Moon," said the eagle.

"Moon, huh? And who sent you?" Charlie asked again, getting very irritated.

"Why do I have to repeat myself? Listen-To-The-Wind!"

To Charlie's amazement, the eagle flapped its wings, took off over his shoulder into the room, and flew unsteadily straight into the open closet. The clang of coat hangers rang out as the small bird smashed against them. It lay there semi-conscious, covered in clothes. Rushing over to the closet, Charlie heard the sound of urgent fluffy woolen slippers on the stairs. He quickly scooped up the eagle and dived into bed, hiding Moon under the covers, just microseconds before his father flung open the door. Cecil Ramsbottom clicked on his flashlight and scanned the room for any unusual signs.

"Charlie, what's going on in here?" asked Mr. Ramsbottom, walking into the room, adjusting his thick, giraffe-patterned glasses. Charlie scrunched up his eyes so he could watch his father's investigation through his knit blanket. Mr. Ramsbottom's flashlight fell on the re-wrapped package. Satisfied it was safe, he tucked his son's blankets tightly into the bed and had just turned away to leave the bedroom, when Charlie felt the eagle struggle to get out from under the covers, its voice squeaking desperately.

"Let me out of here, I can't breathe. I'm getting hot, let me out!" Mr. Ramsbottom did a sharp about turn. Charlie lay still, holding the eagle's nosy beak very tightly and began muttering incoherently, pretending that he was having a nightmare to cover the eagle's urgent pleading.

"Let me out, let me in, undo the ropes, release me, it's so hot, I can't breathe...(snore) zzzzzz." Mr. Ramsbottom shrugged his shoulders and left the room. Charlie kept hold of Moon's beakish nose; not daring to let the eagle go because he knew his father liked playing tricks. Just then, the door swung back open and Mr. Ramsbottom stood there, maneuvering the huge flashlight like the beam from a lighthouse, once again looking for any suspicious activity while Charlie tried with all his might to stop the eagle from wriggling free.

"Just testing, just testing," said Mr. Ramsbottom as he closed the door. Immediately, Charlie pulled back the covers. The eagle sucked in air like a hungry vacuum cleaner and then exploded with the power of a hurricane.

"Well, thank you very much! I travel 10,000 eagle hops with a very important message for a certain Mr. Charlie Ramsbottom and what does he do when he meets me? What does he do, I ask you? He tries to suffocate me under the covers of his very own bed. That's it. I've had enough. I'm leaving."

Moon stood up, eagle-hopped onto the bedside table and started to climb out of the window. But when he saw what was hurt-speeding towards him out of the night sky, he screamed, and jumped back into Charlie's bed and hid, moaning under the same suffocating covers he had just complained about.

"Snarlies! The Snarlies are coming to get me! Shut the windows!" squawked the terrified eaglet. Charlie couldn't understand what Moon was talking about. He went to the window and shone his light through the branches of the huge mango tree. The tree parted its leafy camouflage so Charlie could get a better view. But still, he could see nothing. He was just about to turn back to Moon and ask what all the commotion was about when, from a long way away, he heard a terrible, piercing, ugly noise, a noise that could only be described as a whining, wheezing and sniffling, like someone with a really rotten cold.

Charlie peered out of the window trying to see where the awful racket was coming from. Then two dark dragonish shadows flew across the face of the moon trailing a slimy jet stream. The midnight specters banked and headed towards the farmhouse, partially hidden by a cloud of black smoke. Their noise grew so loud that Charlie had to put his hands over his ears. The pressure in his head glued him to the spot and when he peered out further into the night, he saw four enormous bloodshot eyes breaking through the grime, dive-bombing straight towards him. The ruckus was almost unbearable. Sweat trickled down the back of his neck as the two black streaks descended closer, their whining and sniffling so frightening that Charlie thought his days were numbered.

From behind Charlie, Moon screamed, "Close the window! Close the window!" But it was too late. The wretched pair of Snarlies drew nearer to the mango tree. The tree sensed the danger and closed its branches to protect Charlie but was no match for the Snarlies, who blasted a huge river of green gooba from their snouts at the woody defender. The gooba hit the branches of the mango tree and crumpled everything in its path to reveal the Snarlies in all their glory: disgustingly stinky and hideously ugly. They were almost upon Charlie. He ducked just in time to watch the two slime-streaks fly over his head, crash into the closet and collapse unconscious.

"Dead meat. We're dead meat. Close the doors. Close the doors!" yelled Moon from under the covers. Grabbing his flashlight, Charlie ran over to the closet, but before slamming the doors shut (being the curious kind of boy he was) he could not resist looking at the two large gruesome birds that were lying at the bottom of his closet, momentarily stunned, smelling like rotting cabbage with steamy, green, gooba-gunge dribbling from their snouts. Visibly shaken, Charlie shone his flashlight at the revolting intruders, revealing that they were wearing leather jackets, with chunky silver chains hanging from them; dirty jeans to their knees; large black hobnail boots; and silver crash helmets, which had long red rattlesnakes drawn on the top with the initials S.W. engraved on the side in lime green lettering.

Charlie stood staring at the red rattlesnakes and the S.W. on the trespassers' helmets. He remembered the S.W. etched into the rusty chain around the little eagle's leg. What did the letters mean? He racked his brains. His skin started to itch. Underneath what appeared to be a calm exterior, Charlie Ramsbottom was in one enormous panic. He felt as though his chest would explode and all the time Moon was crying out for him to lock the wardrobe doors. Then it came to Charlie. He made the connection and instantly, a shiver ran down his spine. S.W. stood for...Skunk Weavel; the same name that had appeared on the storybook's cover. As he blurted out "Skunk Weavel," someone tapped him on the shoulder and he nearly jumped out of his skin. He spun around. It was Penelope.

"Skunk Weavel? What are you up to now, Creep-Boy?" she sneered inquisitively, peering over Charlie's shoulder at the unusual creatures in the closet.

"None of your business, vomit breath! Get lost!" But Penelope was intrigued.

"Oh, sick! Wicked! Horror movie! I just love monsters. What kind are they?" she asked, pushing Charlie aside and stepping into the closet to take a closer look. Charlie could hear their father slowly climbing the stairs again.

"Don't tell. I mean it." Mr. Ramsbottom was nearing the top of the stairs.

"Don't give me orders. It's like this Creep, give me your skateboard or no deal," hissed Penelope, engrossed by the Snarlie's appearance.

"Never," said Charlie. Penelope chuckled to herself.

"Well then, it's simple," she hissed. "I'll tell Dad."

Boy! Was she a nasty piece of work! Charlie's hand balled into a fist ready to punch his sister out, but an even better idea stopped him. He froze his hand in mid-air and instead ran his fingers through his hair and smiled.

"You're not scared of these gross monstery things, are you Penelope?" Mr. Ramsbottom was on the landing, almost at the door.

"Haven't found one to scare me yet, Creepoid," she said rather boastfully.

"What do you think they are?" asked Charlie innocently as Penelope grabbed his flashlight. She shone the light on the Snarlies and her attention became so fixed on the creatures that she was totally unaware that her brother had closed the closet door and locked her in.

The bedroom door swung open. Mr. Ramsbottom towered in the doorway, peered around and shone his huge flashlight straight at Charlie's face.

Charlie held his breath, watching his father out of the corner of his eye and, at the same time, listening to the astounding snoring sound that was coming from under his bed-covers.

Chapter Three: Escape from the Snarlies

Of course, it was Moon who was making the snoring noise, so Charlie started to snore even louder to cover the bird's awful din. He put his hands straight out in front of him and walked, like a zombie, back to his bed. When his legs touched the blanket's edge, Charlie slowly lowered his arms to his side and gradually slid into its cozy warmth, enabling him to hide Moon from his father's searching eyes. Cecil Ramsbottom smiled to himself. He had never heard his son snore so loudly.

"Well, I never," he exclaimed. "The wee boy snores just like his mother and even sleepwalks like her. Would you believe it?" Chuckling to himself, he left the room and went downstairs to crank up the generator so he could restore power to the house and, more importantly, continue watching *Talk with the Animals.*

Charlie cradled Moon in his arms. The bird's snores were almost deafening and although Charlie tried to awaken him, the snoring grew louder and louder. Somehow, Charlie had to stop the racket, otherwise Mr. Ramsbottom would be back up the stairs in no time at all. Charlie shook Moon again but his snoring grew even louder, so loud that the window was rattling, the bookshelf was shaking, and the bed was banging against the wall. It was excruciating!

Charlie ran to the closet and checked that the door was still locked. The only sound from the Snarlies was a gurgling snot-filled wheezing, and he could just hear Penelope talking to herself, totally unaware of her plight. As quick as a flash, Charlie strapped his schoolbag across his chest and slipped *The Book of Dreams* and the little eagle inside. Then he carefully climbed out of the window and down the rickety, wooden trellis. As he neared the bottom, Charlie thought he heard the mango tree whimpering and talking to itself. But no, it couldn't be. A mango tree couldn't be talking as well. Could it?

The moment his feet touched the ground, Charlie ran and hid under an enormous macadamia tree that sat on a hill overlooking the plains, down to the sea. From the hilltop, Charlie could make out the lights of passing ships on the horizon. He gazed up at the night sky. It was so clear he could see millions of stars. He felt that if he reached out, he would be able to touch the Milky Way.

Moon's snoring continued to grow in intensity and Charlie needed to get as far away from his parent's listening ears as he could. He decided to head for the garage so he cut across the lawn, using a huge pile of logs for cover. Reaching into the bag, he put his hand over the eagle's mouth and nose, but no matter what he did, Charlie couldn't stop Moon from making that awful harrumbling.

Right then, the power was restored. The house lights flickered into life and Sylvia joined her husband on the front porch to see what the strange noise was. Charlie moved quickly and made his way to the shelter of the garage. Reaching the garage door, Charlie's bathrobe got snagged on an old climbing rose bush, which had made the garage walls its home. Charlie did a double take. The roses hanging from the bush looked wrong. Charlie picked one and its texture felt like chocolate. Smooth, silky. He took a little bite—oh wow, it was chocolate! Such a heavenly taste. Breaking off a small piece from one of the chocolate roses, he pushed it into Moon's mouth. The snoring stopped immediately.

Satisfied that nothing was amiss, Charlie's parents went back inside the house. As they disappeared from view, the sleepy bird started to quietly choke. Suddenly, he awoke and spat the piece of chocolate straight into Charlie's face.

"What are you trying to do, you fool?" cried Moon.

"I was trying to stop you from snoring. It was waking up the whole neighborhood." The bird drew closer to Charlie's face, so close that they were almost touching. Gritting what teeth he had, Moon fired off a salvo at Charlie.

"I've known you for all of ten minutes and already you've tried to kill me twice. Our relationship will have to change if we are to have any chance of succeeding." Charlie felt the tiniest pang of guilt.

"What were you trying to feed me anyway?"

"A piece of chocolate from the rose bush," said Charlie.

For a brief second Moon look confused.

"Well, then at least give me a bigger piece!" demanded the bird. Charlie reached over to the chocolate bush and pulled off another "rose."

Moon put the piece of chocolate between his claws and was just about to take a huge bite when, from the bottom of the hill, there came an enormous groan, a gigantic plop, and a humungous splash. Moon jumped with fright.

"It's alright," said Charlie. "It's just an egg being hatched. That's why it's called Thunder Egg Farm—the chickens." Looking confused, Moon took a bite of his chocolate.

Charlie explained, "When I was born, my father celebrated by going fishing on Lake Plenty. He reckons it must have been a pretty special day because from the bottom of the lake, he pulled up a basket with huge eggs in it. He brought the eggs home and my mother looked after them until they hatched: Thunder Egg Chickens we called them. They grew and grew until they were about twice the size of normal chickens. No one had seen a Thunder Egg Chicken for years; most people thought they were extinct, and they almost were, but now Thunder Egg Farm is a safe haven for them. Those noises just mean that another Thunder Egg has been safely laid."

"I thought it was a Snarlie searching for me," replied a relieved Moon through a mouthful of chocolate.

"I think you'd better tell me why you're here," said Charlie. "I've got to go to school tomorrow, and it's getting late." Moon finished off his chocolate, wiped his nose-like beak, closed his eyes for a few seconds and then spoke in a whisper.

"Listen closely and listen carefully. I'm only going to say

this once. Listen-To-The-Wind...." Charlie rolled his eyes. He'd heard all this before when the bird first appeared at his window ledge.

"Are you going to pay attention to me or not?" demanded Moon. Charlie nodded.

"As I said, Listen-To-The-Wind is the head of our convocation, and he's also a very wise bird. He's my father. He's the one who sent me with the message." Just as Moon took a breath, a cold breeze whistled through his feathers. His head jerked up. Standing silhouetted in Charlie's bedroom window was a pair of dark figures. Moon put his head inside Charlie's bag and began to whimper.

"What's the matter, what's wrong?" asked Charlie.

"It's the Snarlies. They've gotten out of the closet. Hide me. Quickly," cried Moon.

"I bet that snitch Penelope helped them. She'd do anything to hang out with real-life monsters." As if on cue, Penelope appeared at the window between the two evil-looking, dragonesque birds.

"Hurry up, Ramsbottom, we've no time to lose," squawked Moon.

"Who are these Snarlies?" asked Charlie.

Moon squawked even more. "Hide me, quickly, hide me. There's no saying what they'll do if they catch me. Don't you see? They know I've escaped."

"Escaped? Why? What's going on?" asked Charlie, his eyes the size of saucers.

"No time for that now. Hide me, quick! I'll tell you all about it later...if I'm still alive!" Moon looked so fearful that at first,

Charlie didn't know what to do or where to go. He could hear the Snarlies starting to whine. Their appalling sound ran right through the marrow of his bones. Then he had an idea, a brilliant one. Clutching the bag, he fled like lightning down the hill towards the Thunder Egg Chicken coop. As Charlie ran, his foot hit a stone, his legs became entangled like cooked spaghetti and before you could say squidgely-widgely, he and Moon were tumbling tail over teakettle down the hill until they rolled to a stop just outside the main gate of the chicken coop. There, two old, black and brown, matronly Thunder Egg Chickens stood on guard. Charlie looked at the chickens. He rubbed his eyes. Then he pinched himself. No longer were the birds double the size of normal chickens, they were now as big and tall as he was, taller even!

"Charlie, what are you doing down here at this time of night?" enquired Snoozeball, one of the nightwatch-chickens.

Charlie was stunned. The chicken was speaking!

"Listen...ummm...Miss Chicken." Charlie didn't know how to address chickens, let alone giant chickens.

"Snoozeball is my name and this is Runningmouth," said the oversized hen pointing to her companion. Charlie couldn't believe what he was hearing but he didn't have much time to process it, so he told the chickens his problem.

"Snoozeball. You've got to help me. You see those large gruesome figures standing on my window ledge?" Snoozeball nodded as Charlie continued. "They're Snarlies and they're after a friend of mine."

"Oh dear! Snarlies. What an awful nuisance. I'm sure one of them rather looks like your sister, Penelope. How terrible for you. But what friend do you mean?" said Snoozeball, rather unconcerned and yawning at the same time.

"Say, yeah, what friend, what friend, indeed what friend, who's got a friend, I don't see any friend?" dribbled Runningmouth.

"Be quiet dear, would you?" said Snoozeball in a gentle but firm tone. "Now Charlie, what friend are you referring to?" continued Snoozeball. Moon called out from inside the schoolbag.

"*I'm* the friend, you goons," shouted Moon. "And if you don't *do* something soon those Snarlies will have your guts for garters, so *hurry*."

"This is Moon," said Charlie when Moon stuck his head out of the satchel. Upon seeing Moon, Snoozeball and Runningmouth curtsied in the most dignified respect.

"Your Eagleness. We've been expecting you," said Snoozeball.

"Eagleness?" Charlie looked at Moon.

"It's a chick thing," said the bird.

Runningmouth stood up from her curtsy and turned to Snoozeball, whispering, "As Bizz-Buzz predicted. Look at his beak, his beak. It isn't very fierce, is it? Is it?" Snoozeball looked sadly at Moon and said, "It's not a beak at all, it's a nose. Ohhh!" She stroked Moon's head. Both Thunder Egg Chickens felt sorry for the little eagle with the peculiar face.

Charlie could feel Moon's impatience. "Snoozeball, could you hurry up a little, please?"

"Follow us, Charlie," ordered Snoozeball, stifling a yawn. "We'll hide you in the dormitory."

The two chickens opened the large wire gates and led Charlie and Moon down a long, winding flight of stairs that seemed to go on forever. Finally, they reached a bulky swing door, with a huge sign that read:

THUNDER EGG DORMITORY

Although Charlie had lived on Thunder Egg Farm all his life, he had been too scared to enter the chicken coop before because of the size of the chickens. How silly that seemed now with the chickens taking on gigantic proportions. Walking through the doorway, Charlie gazed around the candle-lit coop, astonished. The air was thick with a soft down—it was almost snowing feathers. And the soft clucking of the sleeping chickens created an incredibly drowsy feeling. Charlie rubbed his eyes, hardly believing what he was seeing. In front of him were rows and rows of chickens, all fast asleep in bunk beds attached to the wall. There was a playpen in one corner with an assortment of toys for baby chicks. Opposite to where the chickens slept, stood a long, wooden kitchen table that seated all the birds at meal times. And, on a wall above the table was a large flat-screen TV where the chickens could watch their favorite programs as they prepared to lay their eggs.

Snoozeball turned off *Talk with the Animals* with the remote. The silence was suddenly broken by a distinct noise that filled the coop. It came from a large tub of water, where a new Thunder Egg bobbed about on its way to a box from where Mr. Ramsbottom would collect it in the morning. Snoozeball picked up a large quilted bedspread. "Hide in one of the beds and put this over you," she said. Gripping his bag, Charlie climbed with Moon into one of the spare beds and pulled up the quilt. Snoozeball and Runningmouth sat at the long table, eating rice pudding and drinking hot chocolate. Runningmouth pulled out a pack of cards from under her feathers and gave them a long shuffle. Dealing two hands, she and Snoozeball became a picture of concentration as they started to play.

"I just love playing Happy Families, don't you?" said Snoozeball, taking a swig of her hot chocolate.

"Hey, you're talking to the best darned player in the whole dormitory, if not the whole world," replied Runningmouth as she laid the pair of Mr. & Mrs. Bun the Baker. "I am *so* unbeatable."

"Well, don't be so quick to be humble. Here's Mr. and Mrs. Plod the Policeman." Snoozeball and Runningmouth both laughed out loud.

Charlie and Moon hid under the bedspread and pretended to be asleep, but Moon felt as though he was being suffocated again and rose for air. The young eagle was about to reprimand Charlie for the third time that night, when Snarlie boots could be heard crunching, grating and screeching to a halt on the gravel path overhead. Sniffling and snuffling and arguing with each other, the winged monsters began their search for Moon. The clatter of the Snarlies and their snot-choked gasps moved closer and closer to the stairway that led down to the coop. Charlie heard the familiar voice of his sister Penelope, leading them down to the chicken dormitory. Betrayer!

Too soon, leather steel-toe capped boots smashed against squeaky wooden stairs. Charlie's heartbeat quickened. Runningmouth stopped chattering. Snoozeball gazed wide-eyed at the door while pocketing the pack of cards. Moon dived under the covers and held his breath.

Slowly, the door creaked open. Two long beaks and four bloodshot eyes slimed around the edge of the door. A gloom spread through the coop. There, arrayed in all their black leather gear, were the two largest, fattest, ugliest-looking birds Charlie had ever seen. Their long stubbly-haired skinny legs disappeared into huge, black hobnail boots. One of the Snarlies was gorging on a purpley red-striped piece of fruit. The other one took a live rodent from his coat; put it in his mouth and started to chew. The rat's tail and hind legs wiggled on the outside of his mouth until the Snarlie gulped down the last pieces and licked his beak clean. Then in unison, both Snarlies put on wrap-around sunglasses. Standing behind the pair was a smirking Penelope. To Charlie's dismay, his precious skateboard was dangling from her grasp.

"I don't think my pea-brain brother would be so clever or so brave as to hide down here, Mr. Snarlie, but it's worth a try," she sang off-key. One of the Snarlies raised his right leg in the air and a thunderous sound, like a herd of wild pigs snorting and rampaging through the forest, burst forth from his leather shorts followed by the most awful smell. (This revolting smell and sound was to become known as a Ferocious Attack of the Roaring Trumpets.) The Snarlie snarled and turned on Penelope who reeled backwards from the awful stench. Very slowly, he pulled his finger from his snout and flicked, like a sling-snot, a ball of his slimy gooba at her. The gooba flew through the air with the intensity of a whip's lash and wrapped itself around Penelope, leaving her momentarily stunned. "Aw, sick," she said, at once grossed out and awestruck. Then the Snarlie brought his leg down and kicked the door closed, slamming it in Penelope's stunned face. Now she was locked outside the dormitory, and Charlie and Moon were inside— trapped.

Chapter Four: Happy Families

Petrified, Charlie peaked out from under the covers as the Snarlies stood inside the door growling like two old rusty car exhausts. One of them wore a 70s studded disco belt while the other had a two-way radio, which crackled with static. Snoozeball made the first move. She pulled out the pack of Happy Family cards that she'd put in her coat pocket. Runningmouth gave a gasp of delight and spoke loudly and excitedly.

"Aaaahh! Happy Families, my favorite card game. Can I deal? Can I deal? Pleeeaase let me deal, pleeeaase!" Snoozeball smiled to herself and passed the cards to her friend who gave them a special casino-style shuffle that made a long whirring sound. After a few fabulous twists of the wrist, she composed herself and started to deal.

"Stop," boomed a gruff voice from the end of the room. It was one of the Snarlies. Slowly and deliberately, the leather-clad vulture took off his sunglasses so he could see more clearly, but then very quickly put them back on again, because even the low candle-light was too strong for his shifty eyes.

"What are you going to do with those cards?" he demanded. The Snarlies sidled over to the table like a pair of gun-slinging cowboys. The lead Snarlie ripped a pocket flask from his hip that read, *Fire Water*. He took a long swig from the bottle and when he emptied the receptacle, he inhaled and blew out blue and red flames from his mouth before noisily guzzling down the remaining bowls of rice pudding and hot chocolate.

"Who wants to know?" asked Snoozeball, rather hoity-toitilly.

"Yes, who wants to know?" echoed Runningmouth bravely, although she had to hold her knees to keep them from knocking.

"The name's Flip and this is my pardner, Flop," said the Snarlie.

"Flip and Flop!" Runningmouth burst out laughing at the names until she saw that the Snarlies were giving her a pretty mean stare and cracking the joints of their claw-knuckles.

"I...I...I mean they're lovely names, beautiful names. I wish my parents had been as kind."

"Runningmouth," said Snoozeball in a school-teacherish sort of way. She turned to the Snarlies, "Won't you sit down Mr. Flip, Mr. Flop?" Snoozeball caught Charlie's eye and gave him a sly wink as the Snarlies moved in. She could smell that these vultures were just as addicted to playing cards as she was. "We're playing Happy Families," said Snoozeball. "But it's probably too childish for you."

"Never heard of it," grunted Flop who looked and sounded as though he made a habit of running into brick walls.

"Ever heard of Go Fish? Old Maid perhaps?" asked Snoozeball as Runningmouth smoothly dealt four hands of cards.

Flip and Flop looked at each other as if Snoozeball was speaking Russian. Snoozeball winked at Runningmouth. "Tell them Runningmouth."

"It's easy, so easy. Just look at your hand and lay down your pairs. Here's Mr. and Mrs. Bun the Baker, see? See? They're a pair. If you don't have a pair, you can take from your *pardner's* hand." The Snarlies still looked confused.

"Shall we begin?" asked Snoozeball as she caught Flop looking at Runningmouth in a romantic kind of way.

"Just hold your horses there, Henny Penny," said Flip. "We play on one condition and one condition only."

"And that is…?" asked Snoozeball, fluttering her eyes at the ugly bird.

"If you win, we'll go, but if we win, well, you'll suffer the quincequonces."

"Don't you mean the 'consequences'?" inquired Runningmouth.

"That's what he said, cutie pie, the quincequonces," gargled Flop as he drooled over Runningmouth.

"O.K., O.K. We understand, we understand," said Snoozeball. "Let's get on with it."

The Snarlies sat with their backs to Charlie and Moon as Runningmouth dealt the cards and the game began. Incredibly wrong looking, Flip and Flop were also very shortsighted. When they took out magnifying glasses to look at the cards, Runningmouth began to laugh again but Snoozeball stopped her just in time. And as hand after hand was dealt, it soon became apparent that the Snarlies were definitely the worst card players in the whole universe. Snoozeball and Runningmouth knew that they could thrash these two posers, but prepared themselves for a long night of honorable cheating in order to help Charlie and Moon avoid detection.

All the while, boy and bird peered out from under the bedspread, watching the game while Flip criticized Flop's every mistake with phrases like: "you stupid ignoramus," "you piece of worm's breath," "you most vile work of a nitwit's friend."

"Mr. Plod the Policeman," shouted Flip excitedly, throwing the card down on the table.

"Yes and this makes the pair...Mrs. Bun the Baker," said an almost animated Flop. Flip's face turned a livid shade of red and he started to hit Flop around the head with his leather gloves.

"You fool. Mistakes, mistakes, mistakes. Get out of here. Go up top and make sure nothing gets past you. Just wait until Master Skunk hears about this."

At the mention of Skunk's name, a bell rang in Charlie's brain. In an instant, the Snarlies whipped around, but Charlie and Moon had dived under the covers.

"That's funny, Flop," said Flip, "I'm sure I heard a bell ringing just now. Must be your brain rattling, you feeble excuse for a Snarlie. Now go on, off with you!" Flop trundled over to the doorway feeling rather sorry for himself. He opened the door and looked back longingly at Flip. A trail of steamy gooba drizzled down from his left nostril. Then his gaze turned to Runningmouth. It was the kind of gaze that said, *Hey baby.*

Are you free?! Runningmouth smiled back with the kind of smile that said, *You've got gooba running down your left nostril, dude and it makes you look really handsome.*

"Get out of here, you miserable piece of dried chewing gum!" yelled Flip.

Flop closed the door behind him and shambled up the stairs to the gates of the coop. He was so humiliated that he didn't see Penelope who was standing there in raptures, pulling gooba from her hair like melted cheese from a pizza. She chewed on a piece of the snot-like gunge, "Ooh, gooba! Wicked! Sick! Tastes really salty!"

The game continued and the underground bunker gradually took on an atmosphere of anticipation. The whole chicken coop was awake and sitting on the edge of their tailfeathers to see how the game would unfold. Eventually, on a signal from Snoozeball, and holding the bag very still, Charlie climbed out of the bed and crept along in the flickering shadows until they reached the door. Flip was really enjoying himself as he threw down the last card and shouted with delight that he had won. He jumped up and down hugging and cheering for himself.

"I'm a clever Snarlie, I'm a clever Snarlie. Chickens can't beat Snarlies, nah-nah, nee-nah-nah." And then he started to sing in a voice not even a mother could love:

We are the Snarlies, the Snarlies yous hens,
We'll keep on playing 'til we get to the end

In spite of the horrific screeching, Snoozeball and Runningmouth encouraged Flip to sing on. In his own eyes, he was becoming a singing icon, a TV star in the making, a celebrity.

We are the Snarlies, I'll say it again

Charlie saw his chance. He undid the bolt of the door. S-q-u-e-a-k-i-l-y, s-q-u-e-a-k-i-l-y, the rusty door began to whine as it opened. Runningmouth immediately covered for Charlie by letting out the most enormous high-pitched squeal, encouraging Flip's singing prowess.

"Oh dear, this is the first time ever we've been beaten. Ever! How are we going to face the other chickens, Runningmouth?" said a teary Snoozeball. Flip's head grew bigger on his shoulders. "The cards must have been rigged," she continued. "We just have to admit it. We've finally met our match!" But Flip was so involved in his moment of glory that he just kept belting out the song:

We're very bad losers
We just like to win!

By the time Flip had finished his song and calmed down, Charlie and Moon were outside the door ready to rush back to Charlie's bedroom. Charlie crept over to where Penelope was now playing with her gooba, like Silly Putty, grabbed his skateboard and smiled at Penelope's muted protestations. Then he and Moon were gone, rushing up the stairs that led to the farmyard.

Inside the dormitory, Flip issued an ultimatum, "You know why we're here," he said. Snoozeball and Runningmouth shook their heads. "We've come for Moon. Where is he?" he continued, clenching his claws.

"Come for the moon?" repeated Snoozeball innocently, pointing out the chicken house window at that celestial orb.

"Not *the* moon. MOON! He's here," said Flip. "We've been searching for him for 10,000 eagle hops. I know he's here. I can smell him. Where is he?"

"Look," said Runningmouth, "You, you, you come in here at this late hour, beat my friend and me at Happy Families and then demand to see a character called Moon. The only moon you'll find around here is the one up in the sky outside. Your question just doesn't make sense. So chill baby, chill!"

"Listen here you fluffy old chook, I want that eagle. If you don't give him to me, I'll take you to Skunk Weavel, and then you'll be in real trouble and suffer the quincequonces." Runningmouth began to correct Flip's pronunciation but Snoozeball quickly prevented her from speaking, she could see that the Snarlie was becoming extremely hostile. Starting to stream hot gooba from his enormous nostrils, Flip continued his demand.

"You've got ten seconds to change your mind." The countdown began slowly and thoughtfully.

"Ten-eight-four..."

Right at that moment, Charlie and Moon had reached the top of the stairs, looking behind them every few steps in case they were being followed. Charlie stopped, paused for breath, and leaned against the wall, panting.

"We're safe for the moment," he said to Moon. "We should go to the garage. We can hide in the car, and you can tell me what's going on." Moon nodded in agreement.

Meanwhile, back in the coop, the countdown was continuing.

"Six-three-eight-," drawled Flip trying to appear menacing but only sounding dense. He was just as bad at counting as he was at cards.

At the gates of the chicken coop, Charlie was about to run up the hill to the garage when a vice-like claw gripped him very tightly by the shoulders. Charlie looked around. It was Snarlie-bird Flop. "Gotcha," hissed Flop with delight. From the schoolbag, Moon screamed indignantly at Flop.

"Let him go! He's an innocent! Let him go!" With a great sense of delight, Flop replied, "Shut up your stinkiness, or I'll eat you...your most gracious smelliness. Wait 'til The Toyminator gets his hands on you. Ha, ha, ha!"

Flop quickly frog-marched a scared-stiff Charlie down the stairs towards the dormitory door, holding a screaming Moon upside down by a leg. When the Snarlie reached the door, it was locked, so he propped both Charlie and Moon face against the wall.

"Don't move, none of you!" Flop was so excited and proud of himself that he turned away from his prisoners and banged as hard as he could on the door, completely unaware that Flip was counting down the Thunder Egg Chickens on the inside.

"Four-two-seven-,"

Bang! Crash! Bang!

Inside the hen house, Flip stopped counting when he heard the commotion from outside. In a flash, he unlatched the bolt and tried to push the door open. Each Snarlie pushed as hard as he could knowing that he was being watched and that he would have to win to show how tough he was.

While Flop was trying to prove his super Snarlie strength, Charlie leaned against a piece of wood by the door and a secret panel in the wall started to slide open before their astonished eyes. Stunned by their luck, Charlie and Moon turned and looked at Penelope, both gagging at the sight of her. After a moment's consideration, they looked at each other and in unison said, "No Way!" Charlie picked up Moon, put him back inside the bag, jumped on his skateboard and pushed off down the dark tunnel, leaving Penelope behind.

Flop, still pushing with all his might, wasn't aware of what was happening behind him. And a trail of gooba was oozing from his snout onto the floor. Teetering off balance, his feet slipped in the green gunge and he lost his grip. Suddenly, the door burst open and Flip flew through the air to land spread-snarlied on the ground next to Flop, who stood up, very proudly, opposite the doorway. He had a look on his face, which said, *Aren't I a clever Snarlie?*

"Look who I've got," said Flop, as chirpily as he could.

Behind the Snarlies, the panel was starting to close. Charlie and Moon were disappearing around a corner in the secret passageway. They dared not look back.

"Who have you got?" said an indignant Flip, spitting out the words one at a time.

"Why, Moon and the kid. That's who." Flop grinned and turned to look at Charlie and Moon—but they were gone. Slowly, Flop swiveled around to gawp at Flip whose face had turned a bright volcanic purple. Together, the birds stared at the secret doorway, which was at that moment, inching to a close.

"Run after them you fool. Run!" shouted Flip to Flop. Both Snarlies rushed to the panel and managed to squeeze through the tiniest of spaces just before it grated to a close. The chase was on!

Chapter Five: Breakfast in Bed

In no time at all, the Snarlies began to gain on Charlie and Moon. Charlie stopped for a moment to listen for the interlopers and although he couldn't see Flip and Flop, he could hear their awful sound drawing closer. The Snarlies were almost upon them, so close now that you could virtually smell their horrible stinky breath. And their whine was enough to make anyone shiver to death. In the darkness, Charlie raced blindly along the tunnel. Screaming out to Moon that he could hardly see, the skateboard hit some loose rocks and Charlie and the bird smashed headlong into the ground. The Snarlies hurtled through the darkness and screeched to a halt. As they started to move in on Charlie and Moon, Flip screamed out, "I can smell fresh meat. Time to eat. NOW!" Charlie looked at Moon and whispered, "I don't want to be eaten!" The snarling Snarlies towered above them, noisily sniffing the scent of their prey.

Slime dribbled from their beaks. Flop reminded Flip why they were there. "What about the book, Flip?"

"Don't remind me, you idiot, of course I know that," Flip said, sweating inwardly and not wanting to admit he had forgotten the most important part of his mission. "Give us the book. Then we'll eat you." As he spoke, a shaft of the earliest pre-dawn light began pouring in through an opening just above them, exposing the Snarlies in all their ugly glory.

Suddenly, Moon started to laugh out loud, hardly able to contain himself.

"The light," he squawked merrily. "They hate the light." The small ray of light was getting brighter by the minute.

"Can't get us, can't get us. Nah-nah, nee-nah nah. Nah-nah, nee-nah nah," Moon teased the two gruesome critters. Charlie didn't know what to make of Moon's actions but was equally surprised when the Snarlies started to shake.

"The light weakens their nervous system and eventually turns them into mush," said Moon. "If they don't get back to their lair before sun-up, they'll be mince meat through the grinder. Nah-nah, nee-nah nah. Who's a stupid Snarlie? Flip and Flop, they look like snot!" shouted Moon. He was really enjoying himself making Skunk Weavel's pair of hench-birds grit their beaks.

"We'll return and we'll get you, you mangy maggot," shouted Flip. On that note, the two shortsighted, stubbly-legged birds tore off down the passageway looking for a way out. Charlie felt the blood rush to his head. His heart surged inside his chest. Quite unexpectedly, he let out a blood-curdling scream.

"After them!" he yelled and set off in hot pursuit of the Snarlies.

"No," cried Moon "Just let them go." But it was too late. Charlie was already gaining on the Snarlies with poor Moon bouncing up and down inside the satchel. They could hear Flip and Flop nearing an opening in the tunnel that led to the top of the stairs. The sound of Flip's two-way radio crackled through the crisp morning air. Rounding a tight corner, Charlie almost crashed into the gruesome birds, but just managed to stop before Flip and Flop saw him. Suddenly realizing he wasn't so brave, by the fact that his legs started to feel like jelly on springs, Charlie quickly hid in a recess in the wall. He heard a voice come across Flip's radio. In a snide, hissing tone, it said, "You have failed, Bird-Brain. Return to Weavel Headquarters for your punishment or I'll wilt you at sunrise, you flaky fleck of a dried-up tea bag." Then Charlie and Moon could hear Flip sniffling and berating Flop as the two birds moved out into the soft pre-dawn light to prepare for their journey back to Skunk Weavel's. They watched the Snarlies arguing with each other and then witnessed the most perilous of take-offs.

The Snarlies were so out of shape that it took them three attempts to rise up from Thunder Egg Farm. Each time they tried to ascend into the morning sky, their wheezing got louder and louder, pulling them back to earth. Eventually they climbed, grumbling and whining to the top of a rubber tree, unceremoniously bent a large limb back with their weight and then waited for gravity and the laws of physics to toss them into the air. Almost instantly, the rubber tree catapulted the Snarlies high into the clouds and they flew straight up until they were mere specks to the naked eye. At the top of their trajectory, they paused for a moment and started to descend rather rapidly. Only then were they able to move into hurt-speed, immediately banking into a flight path that would return them to the Toyminator's dark world.

Together, Charlie and Moon watched the flight path of Flip and Flop until they were dots in the sky, a sky that was illuminated by the beautiful iridescent yellowy-golden warmth of the sun slowly rising from behind the hill on which Thunder Egg farmhouse stood. In the still morning air, from a great distance Flip could be heard castigating his partner as they merged with the day.

"It's your fault Flop, all your fault. If I die, if I wither, you'll get it. The master is going to be very, very unhappy with you, you sniveling excuse for camel's spit." Then they finally disappeared off the radar.

At the same time, Clarence, the farm rooster, signaled the new day with a large and throaty rap-like cock-a-doodle-doo. He sang:

It's time for you to rise
It's time for you to groove
To get up off your perch
And cock-a-doodle do!
Shake it to the left
Shake it to the right
Do that funky chicken
And cluck with all your might!

Before Clarence could finish his Motown special, a host of

other birds joined in and Moon, temporarily forgetting his troubles, began to warble as only a young eagle can.

As the song came to an end, Clarence called out to the coop, "This Rooster is leaving the henhouse! O Lordy Lordy girls…"

Charlie tapped Moon on the shoulder and said, "We'll have to go back to the house. It's my birthday and Mum's going to bring breakfast into my room in about five minutes. If I'm not there, I'll be in big trouble."

"O.K. birthday boy," said Moon. "Let's go. The sooner we can set off to save my family, the better." Before Charlie could say anything else, the clanking of cutlery rang out from the farmhouse. Charlie and Moon hurried up the hill towards the garage and then across to the lattice that hugged the wall, all the way up to Charlie's bedroom.

As Charlie scaled the wooden trellis with Moon under his arm, he could hear his parents in the kitchen crooning their daily lovesong to each other, "Drea-ea-ea-ea-eam, dream, dream, dream. When I want you in my arms, when I want you and all your charms, whenever I want you, all I have to do is drea-ea-ea-ea-eam…" Charlie waited until Cecil and Sylvia were in duet, opened the window carefully and stealthily climbed into his bed. He had just closed his eyes when his mother, still humming the song, struggled through the door with a large breakfast tray. Moon stood on the outside windowsill, out of sight of Mrs. Ramsbottom, who put the heavy tray down on the bedside table and kissed Charlie on the cheek.

"Charlie, Charlie, time to get up. Happy birthday!" Charlie made the most enormous yawn and slowly sat up. He grabbed

Bizz-Buzz's package from his pocket and held it close so his mother wouldn't see the torn wrapping paper.

"Hello mum. What time is it?" He pretended to wipe the sleep from his eyes.

"It's 7:30, Charlie, time to have your breakfast and then go to school." Sylvia put the tray on Charlie's lap, closed the window and went downstairs. Charlie looked at the tray. On it was another birthday present–a box wrapped in silvery paper. He started to open it when Moon called out in squeaky tones,

"Let me in. Let me in. I'm hungry, I'm hungry."

Charlie pushed the tray aside, got up and let Moon in. The bird couldn't believe his eyes. There on the tray was a gigantic egg, a Thunder Egg with toasted bread-soldiers, an array of chocolate biscuits, and a huge mug of steaming hot tea. Charlie carefully sliced the top off the Thunder Egg, which was about twice the size of a football, and a flood of yellowy goo began to ooze and slowly gurgle down its sides. He dunked one of the soldiers into the yolk, put it in his mouth and chewed on it like a cow eating grass.

"What about me? Aren't you going to give me any?" whimpered Moon, who was very hungry.

"Not until you tell me why you've come here. I've lost a night's sleep over you, and I've got to go to school today. And I'm going to be very tired. And Mr. Grumblebum my teacher will be...."

"O.K. O.K. Sorry, sorry. Can I have some of that?" the little bird begged, salivating at Charlie's breakfast. "Just a bite, then and I'll tell you the whole story."

Moon slid one of his little wings across Charlie's arm. Charlie smiled and dunked a soldier for Moon who sucked on the toast as if his life depended on it. He made a funny, laughing, gargling noise as it slid down his throat before readying himself for another piece.

"When did you last eat?" enquired Charlie.

"Oh, it must have been at least 10,000 Eagle hops ago," said Moon, trying to get at the chocolate biscuit in Charlie's hand.

"Hey. Hey. Slow down. Eagle hops? I don't understand."

"Well, it takes one turn of the wind to do 1,000 eagle hops and there are ten winds in a day, so it must have been...err...let me see...two times five...minus six...plus four, add another four and subtract two...that's ten turns of the wind ago!"

Totally confused by Moon's reply, Charlie dunked four toasted soldiers in the egg yolk and fed them to Moon, who gobbled the slightly burnt bread down in record time. The eagle's eyes glowed with delight. He jumped off the bed, picked one of Charlie's shirts up off the floor and cleaned the goo from his face. "Hey, that's my best Sunday shirt," said Charlie.

"And I suppose that's why you always leave it on the floor, so it's easy to find," said Moon laughing. After a pause, the little bird drew in his breath, ruffled his feathers and prepared himself for the most important speech of his life.

"This is why I have come." He pointed to his nose.

"What do you mean?" asked Charlie. Moon climbed back onto the bed and slid his legs under the covers.

"Eagles are proud birds. We are the protectors of the skies

and beyond and our responsibility is to guard *The Book of Dreams*."

"What *is* *The Book of Dreams*?" asked Charlie undoing the wrapping paper. "Seems like it's only half a book to me, anyway."

"Excuse me, but I haven't finished." said Moon continuing. "Over the years, the air became so polluted that we could barely breathe and we couldn't see and so, unable to fly, we dropped from the skies and became grounded. Our beaks had to quickly evolve into these ridiculous noses to help us survive." Moon pointed to his nosey beak. "The pollution made us sicker and slower than we realized. And that's how the Snarlies captured us."

"I don't get it," said Charlie.

"One night, while we were all sleeping in the bush, the Snarlies heard our loud snoring. Before we knew what was happening, they threw a huge net over us, we were goobered, packed into wooden crates and taken to the dungeon of Skunk Weavel."

"Skunk Weavel!" shouted Charlie. Moon looked down his straight beaked nose at Charlie again and coughed under his breath as if to say, "I still haven't finished." Charlie gave an apologetic look. Moon continued.

"Without our guardianship, *The Book of Dreams* became vulnerable to attack. If you look in the book, it might show you what happened." Charlie took the book out of its wrapping and carefully opened it. Inside, the damaged pages showed a cloudy night sky. Then there was a glow from within the pages and Charlie saw images appear almost like he was watching a film. "Whoa!" gasped Charlie.

There sitting proudly atop a magnificent oaken table was *The Book of Dreams*, the same one Charlie was holding. An old man with a long beard and a young boy were sitting at the table reading the book. They had their backs to Charlie and he couldn't see who they were. The boy spoke, his voice seeming to answer a previous question.

"If I could have one wish, I'd wish I could..." At that moment a green slime catapulted across *The Book of Dreams* and the very same Snarlies that were now after Charlie and Moon flew into view screeching and trying to grab hold of the book.

"Don't let go!" screamed Charlie, the same way he always yelled at the TV screen during an action movie.

The old man held the book with all his might but the Snarlies were too strong for him. The boy, seeing the old man struggling, fearlessly took hold of the book and fought the two vultures alone.

"Wow," Charlie said, the action mounting.

Charlie and Moon watched as the tug-of-war raged on, with the boy and one of the Snarlies each yanking on the book. The other Snarlie viciously pecked at the boy and dive-bombed him, trying to get him to release his grip. All of a sudden, there was a huge tearing sound and the book ripped in two. From within the pages, Charlie and Moon watched the Snarlies flying off shrieking and laughing with half of the book, obviously thinking that they had gotten what they had come for. *"Won't the Master be pleased!"* they yelled as their voices faded from the pages. The other half remained in the boy's grasp. He gave it to the old man, who looked forlornly down at the ruined volume and then back at the boy, but the boy had vanished.

As the man searched for the boy, he turned to look in the direction of Charlie who sat there gobsmacked. Then the picture swirled into nothingness.

"Hey, snap out of it," said Moon. "If Skunk gets his slimy hands on the whole book, we're done for! He'll be able to manipulate everyone's dreams. And when he does that, he'll be able to control everything! The whole world!"

"Wait! So *The Book of Dreams* protects dreams?"

Moon nodded. "And not just sleeping dreams. It keeps a hold of everyone's deepest wishes and desires. It keeps them safe. If Skunk can put the two parts together, it will be nightmarish, have no doubt."

"Well then, why don't *you* stop him?" asked Charlie.

"Because we are beaten. Skunk made an evil potion to turn every endangered animal into a stuffed toy. And he's feeding the strongest batch to my family tonight! Once all of us are extinct, he'll go after the planet's remaining creatures."

Charlie felt his skin start to itch. Moon continued,

"My father, Listen-To-The-Wind, is a broken eagle. One day, in despair, he was desperately trying to find a solution to our problem, when an old newspaper blew into Skunk Weavel's prison cellar. There was an article about the chickens at Thunder Egg Farm, and how they had been saved from extinction. And, there was a picture of *you* and your family standing outside the chicken coop with some Thunder Egg Chickens."

Excitedly, Charlie cried, "Do you mean that picture?" He pointed to the framed article on the wall next to his calendar.

Moon nodded slowly and continued, "My father recognized something in you and thought if we were able to make contact, there might be a chance. I was sent to find you, because I was the smallest and could climb up through a hole in the wall to escape."

Charlie's skin twitched and itched even more. He scratched himself through his clothing and started to ask what Moon was talking about, when Moon raised a claw and put it to Charlie's lips. The eagle pulled a piece of parchment from his waistcoat pocket. Charlie jumped back. It was bound in the same blue silken cloth and had the same wax seal on it that had bound *The Book of Dreams*. As Moon held the ancient paper in his claw, Charlie's heartbeat quickened. Moon spoke in the gravest of tones: "Only open this message if you are prepared to accept its consequences." Charlie closed his eyes for a moment to think. A voice drifted into his being, a gentle voice that said, *You have been chosen. The eagles need your help. We all need your help. Do your best, and all will be well!* Charlie felt comforted by the strangely familiar voice, opened his eyes, took the weathered parchment from Moon, broke the seal and unfurled it. Then he read the message out loud, a message scratched in royal eagle blood that said:

Decree of the
Royal Blue and Gold Winged Eagle Council
To: Charlie Ramsbottom
You have been chosen to save us!
The eagles need your help,
We all need your help
Do your best and all will be well!

"Unbelievable," whispered a shocked Charlie, realizing that the inner voice had said those very words. It unsettled him. "How do you and your father think I could save your family? I'm only nine years old, NOT some kind of super kid." Moon was quiet for a while.

"We had no other choice, Charlie," said Moon. "We were desperate and saw the newspaper blowing into our prison as a sign from the Eagle Gods."

"You don't understand, do you? It's my birthday today. One of my teachers, Noni Benoni, is throwing a big birthday party for me at school. It's my day!"

"But our best chance is under the cover of daylight. The Snarlies can only attack at night. Please! You *have* to help. My father and mother said that if you were going to help us, a sign would be shown to you. Maybe it's in the book? Please at least take another look."

Reluctantly, Charlie reopened the incomplete *Book of Dreams*. He turned to page nine, which showed the profile of a noble eagle. Suddenly, the eagle in the book started to speak:

You are now responsible for this adventure.
You have two choices.
Do nothing and extinction is imminent.
Or
Reunite The Book of Dreams
and save us and yourself!

Charlie was stunned into silence, his eyes fixed on the words on the parchment. Suddenly, the door burst open. His father stood waiting to take him to catch the bus for his last day of school before the Christmas holidays.

Chapter Six: Show and Tell

"Well happy birthday, my bonny boy. What have you got there?" said a smiling Mr. Ramsbottom. Charlie was just going to explain about Moon, when he realized that his father was staring intensely at the end of the bed. Let it be known that Cecil Ramsbottom was so myopic that he could just about see his fingers in front of his nose. Anyway, by now Moon had become so used to hiding that he had already dived under the covers. Mr. Ramsbottom sat on the edge of the bed (almost squashing Moon) and casually picked up the book. He put on his thick glasses and opened it at random.

"Look Charlie. Thunder Egg Chickens. It says here, these birds were almost extinct until we Ramsbottoms started a home for them here on Thunder Egg Farm. Now the birds are almost a common sight around the Shire." Mr. Ramsbottom proudly patted himself on the back. Charlie could hardly believe his ears. He grabbed the book from his father and read the title: *Rare Birds.* What was going on?

"I think you should give yourself a pat on the back as well, laddie," said his father. Quite numbed, Charlie did as he was told and perfunctorily tapped his own shoulder. While Mr. Ramsbottom continued reading the book, Charlie climbed out of bed and got ready for school.

"Says here that the Royal Blue and Gold winged eagle is becoming extinct...but nobody knows why," said Mr. Ramsbottom, flipping to another page. "It's funny because Bizz-Buzz mentioned that the last time I saw him." Charlie stopped and looked over his father's shoulder at the book. On the page was an eagle that looked exactly like Moon.

"Bizz-Buzz, Bizz-Buzz. Who is this Bizz-Buzz?" Charlie asked, rather gruffly. "It's as if he doesn't exist. How come I've never seen him?" But Cecil Ramsbottom closed the book and changed the subject. "I see you haven't opened your other present yet."

Charlie looked at the small box. He ripped off the silver wrapping paper. Inside was a beautiful conch shell.

"What am I supposed to do with this?" asked Charlie rolling his eyes. Cecil Ramsbottom smiled and hugged his son.

"I'll explain later today when we have your birthday feast," he said. Charlie let out a frustrated groan. He couldn't believe that instead of the new version EM9 that he really wanted, all he got so far was half a book and a shell!

"Ready for school, son?" asked his father cheerfully. Charlie picked up the book and stuffed it in his schoolbag but left the conch on the table by his bed. He waited behind while his father went downstairs then quickly pulled the book out of his bag. The title had reverted to half of the first title and half of the other title; *The Book of Dre... ...unk Weavel Rules.* Moon poked his head out of the covers. He was panting for air.

"Hoi! Don't forget me. Your father nearly killed me when he sat down on the bed. Squashed and suffocated. What a way to go! You and your father are really alike, aren't you?"

But Charlie was completely consumed by what was happening with the book. "Look, look at this. Do you know what happened?" he said pointing to the cover. "The book changed its title so my father wouldn't see *this* title."

"We have to be careful, Charlie," whispered Moon, drawing his new friend back into his reason for being there. "We're dealing with the strangest order of magic here. Your half of the book is trying to match with the half that Skunk Weavel has. The book will present you with different options. It's for you to choose correctly. One wrong move and..."

"Hey, Charlie!" interrupted Mr. Ramsbottom calling from downstairs.

"One wrong move and what?" said Charlie.

His father called out again, "Charlie, hurry up. You'll miss the bus."

"Look Moon, I can't take you to school. You'll have to hang around the farm. We'll discuss this later."

"But my family! What about my family? They're in danger!" cried Moon.

"I've got to go," said Charlie, picking up his skateboard and schoolbag. As Charlie left his bedroom, his mother was gingerly steering a gooba-covered Penelope into her bedroom. Before Sylvia closed the door, Charlie saw her sit his sister down on the bed. Looking through a crack in the door, Charlie watched Sylvia chastise Penelope. "Now young lady, just tell me again what happened. This time I want the truth."

"Alright I'll tell you, I'll tell you. But please save some of this gooba in a jar for me and keep it in the fridge. It's d-lish!" Sylvia shook her head as Charlie caught Penelope's eye and stuck his tongue out at her. She hissed at him but Charlie just smiled and ran out of the house.

From the window ledge, the young eagle watched Mr. Ramsbottom push Charlie off on his skateboard towards the bus stop. Chomping on the yolk-soaked toast, Moon felt a strange twitching in his nose and rubbed his face hard under his wing to rid himself of the irritation. When Charlie reached the bottom of the hill, the little eagle saw the boy throw up his hands in frustration as the red No. 9 bus tore off into the distance with its cool South American music blaring from the windows, leaving Charlie behind. Charlie started to chase the bus and passed the bus stop where an old man was sitting watching. The man tugged worriedly on his long white beard, observing Charlie's skateboard prowess, visibly impressed.

Charlie didn't notice that the old gent was watching him intensely, and flew steadily down the road. Arriving at the crest of the next hill, Charlie stopped for a breath. He waited for a moment and then propelled himself to go where no skateboard or boy had ever gone before. As the skateboard wheels churned against the road, Charlie felt the first few drops of rain hit his face.

Speeding down the hill, he rounded a bend until he came to Waterfall Drop, so named because of its incredibly steep decline. Charlie took a deeper breath and kept going. The rain started to become heavier and thicker, almost blinding him. He passed a sign that read: THUNDER EGG DOWNS VILLAGE. And then the sheets of water started to turn into white snowflakes. Amazed and confused, Charlie looked up at the sky and realized that the snow was falling only on him. But these were no ordinary snowflakes. They were snowflakes with attitude, chasing Charlie and following his every move. They were burning themselves into his skin and gradually getting darker and darker until they became black slime falling out of the sky. At the bottom of Waterfall Drop, Charlie could vaguely see the outline of his school as he sped in through the gates trying to outmaneuver the black snow. Just then, the red No. 9 bus left the school and a woman with a beehive hairdo hung from the deck and waved at him. Looking out of the window at Charlie was the same old man who had been at the bus stop. He smiled hopefully when he saw Charlie fending off the black snow.

As he walked into his classroom, all the children looked and laughed at Charlie, who was covered from head to toe in black slime. "You look like you've been attacked by black gunk," Mr. Grumblebum, the class teacher said calmly, adjusting his red turban. "Here, take this towel and clean yourself up." In no time at all, Charlie was back in the classroom, grateful for the lack of questions and the assistance from his teacher.

Charlie knew that Noni Benoni, the Jamaican school librarian, had made plans to give him a special party. He also knew that it was his turn to show and tell and because he didn't get the brand new EM9 he wanted, he would have to show them the dilapidated old book. He decided he would tell them that he'd been given a wonderful book on rare birds and would then sit down, hoping not to bring any attention to himself.

The whole party thing was a disturbing annoyance for Mr. Grumblebum, the class teacher, who was giving a lesson on how to stay afloat if you ever fell into a raging river. Mr. Grumblebum addressed the class, "So, you've been dragged into the River Googly and you can't swim. What should you do?" Lots of children's hands shot up towards the sky but Charlie just looked out the window.

"Charlie Ramsbottom. What is *your* answer?"

"Err...err...fly?" The entire class broke into laughter. Mr. Grumblebum looked into Charlie's eyes and said, "Stay relaxed." Right at that very moment, Noni Benoni rushed into the classroom looking very perplexed. "We've just had a storm warning. The weather's going to turn bad. I'm afraid we are going to have to cancel your party Charlie." The class groaned and Charlie looked extremely disappointed. "Oh man! I wanted my birthday party. You promised!" Realizing immediately how babyish he sounded, Charlie blushed furiously.

"Why not tell us about your present," suggested Noni, winking at Mr. Grumblebum. Charlie felt reluctant about reading from *The Book of Dreams*. He looked around for inspiration, for a sign and noticed that the branches of the tree outside were straining to reach for the sky. His gaze moved further up the tree. Out of the corner of his eye, Charlie saw a strange movement. Above him, the clouds had moved into position to form three words that read:

Save the eagles

Charlie's jaw dropped. He looked at the waiting children and then back at the sky but the words were gone. Slightly nervous, he took a deep breath and decided to tell the class about the plight of the Blue and Gold Winged eagle. He carefully opened the pages of the book and began speaking, being sure not to mention the Snarlies or Skunk Weavel because that would be dangerous. Instead, what he did say was that the eagles could become extinct because of some unusual goings on. He also said that he had been chosen to help the eagles and that he might have to go on an adventure. Charlie spoke like no child had spoken in that school before and word quickly got around that something special was happening in the classroom.

Very soon all the children and teachers at the school began to crowd into the class. As Charlie continued his tale, the crowd was swelled with passers-by. Even Mr. Grumblebum stood back to listen to Charlie's marvelous story. And that's what they all believed it was, a story.

"What a wonderful tale Charlie, truly wonderful," said Noni Benoni. Everyone agreed.

"But it's not a story, it's the truth!" said Charlie. "Ask Penelope, she'll tell you it's the truth." But Penelope wasn't there because she was at home being de-goobered by her mother.

"It's not a story, it's the truth, I'm telling you!" cried Charlie, as he sat down despondently. "Why don't you believe me?" Charlie sat there with his head in his hands. Nobody would listen. Then he sensed someone was standing in front of him. It was Mr. Grumblebum.

"That's the best story I have ever heard, Charlie. You have a most wonderful imagination," he said in his thick Mumbai accent. Mr. Grumblebum's good humor quickly disappeared, however, as he became the serious teacher person again. He continued. "In fact, so good is your imagination, that I suggest you write it all down this instant, after you've finished work on how to stay afloat in a raging river."

Charlie wondered what Mr. Grumblebum's lesson about staying afloat in a raging river had to do with *him*. There were more important things to consider in this world, but he did as Mr. Grumblebum asked and wrote out the facts in his best handwriting. At least *he* knew his story was true. When the bell rang at lunch time, the rest of the class went to the gym and let go of some of the energy that tends to build up from having to sit in a classroom all morning, doing dreary, boring work. Charlie looked out the window. He reached down and pulled the book from his bag. Opening it, he re-read the message:

You are now responsible for this adventure.
You have two choices.
Do nothing and extinction is imminent.
Or
Reunite The Book of Dreams
and save us and yourself!

He turned to the next page, which showed the morning's proceedings: Moon watching him from the window: his skateboard journey to school: telling his story and no one believing him. As well, written in larger letters was the following message:

Time is running out. You need to hurry, otherwise..

Written in even bigger letters was the following warning:

...The Skunk Weavel Rules!

Underneath the words was a picture of the mouth that had been on the opening page when he first looked at the book. More of the face was revealed now; the bulbous nose, which displayed a colony of fly's legs protruding from each nostril; the thin line of dribble that ran diagonally from the corner of the mouth across and down the pointy chin. And the flakes of dandruff that covered the enormous ears like a blanket of snow. Charlie was dumbstruck. He couldn't believe what he was reading or seeing. It was all too much. He felt his eyes getting a little heavy, so he closed them for a moment to think. He literally thought for the first second, but being so tired from the events of the previous night, he actually drifted off to sleep by the second second. In his brief slumber, Charlie saw himself being engulfed by a huge wall of water. Just as he was about to be pulled under for the last time, he was awakened by a tapping sound and then a familiar voice.

"Wake up, Charlie, wake up; we've got things to do and places to go!" Charlie snapped out of his reverie and gazed out of the classroom window. There was Moon, confidently flapping around. Charlie opened the window and Moon came to rest on the ledge, panting and puffing.

"Well, what do you think?" said Moon, getting his breath back and prancing up and down on the ledge.

"Think of what?" asked Charlie, still a little downcast.

"My nose. Look at my nose. It's become a beak! Isn't it a wondrous turn of events!" Charlie examined Moon's face. Yes, he did have a beak and he looked a little larger and stronger now.

"How, how did it happen?" asked Charlie.

"It must have been the yolk from the Thunder Egg we had for breakfast," said Moon. "I was eagle-hopping around the farm this morning when my nose suddenly started to change into a real beak. What's more, I felt so strong that I actually snapped off that awful chain from my leg. And I can fly like a bird. Look, every minute, I am getting stronger and stronger."

Moon gave a little demonstration, flapping his wings so that he took off momentarily from the window ledge. Upon landing, he called out joyfully, "You know what this means, don't you?" Charlie shook his head, so Moon continued, "It means that we can rescue my family! The yolk from the eggs will turn our noses into beaks, and we won't snore any more, and we'll be able to protect the skies and *The Book of Dreams*, and we'll be extra strong and..." Charlie interrupted his feathered friend.

"That's really great, Moon, really great. But there's just one problem. Your family is 10,000 eagle hops away and the Thunder Eggs are here. Would you like to explain how the eggs are going to get themselves to Skunk Weavel's toy factory?"

"That's easy," said Moon, flipping open the book. "We're

going to take them. I bet it's in here," he said, proudly pointing to the book with his beak. Charlie turned to the next page. It read:

You cannot refuse, Charlie Ramsbottom!

Below the words was also the faintest series of pictures showing Charlie standing on a stretch skateboard with Moon atop his shoulder. Strapped to the board were two Thunder Eggs. The board was speeding out of Thunder Egg Downs towards a desolate place called the Plains of Desire. A signpost pointed the way to the City of the Quincequonces.

"Do you believe me now?" said Moon, happy that he would soon be setting off to save his family. Charlie didn't answer. He was too stunned to speak.

Chapter Seven: Hatching a Plan

Charlie looked at the pictures in utter amazement. There in front of him, lay his destiny. What was he to do? Moon reminded him that they must act quickly because Skunk Weavel was going to turn the eagles into stuffed toys that very night. The blood started to drain from Charlie's face. His clothing seemed to tighten, so he undid his shirt collar. His mouth felt dry and his skin started to itch irritatingly. He was scared. Leaving Thunder Egg Downs had not actually entered his thoughts. He turned to Moon.

"Moon, I can't leave. This is your problem. You came to me, I didn't come to you." He avoided Moon's eyes as the bird looked despairingly at him.

"But the book says you cannot refuse. You are the only hope we have!"

"I've only just turned nine, Moon, just turned nine! And there's no way I can cross the Plains of Desire. I'd never be seen again!" Charlie was very firm and at the same time extremely scared. Moon looked as if he would burst into tears but Charlie held his ground and turned away. From behind him came a flapping sound. Charlie spun around but Moon was gone, disappearing into a huge mass of storm clouds. Just at that moment, the school bell rang and the other children poured back into the classroom.

Charlie was unusually silent in class that afternoon, outwardly absorbing Mr. Grumblebum's lesson, but inwardly searching for the right answer. He was tempted to open the book but his fear stopped him. At one point, he came so close to opening it, he could have sworn that the sound of thunder and a flash of lightning shot out from its pages. Then as Charlie looked out of the window, the heavens literally opened and sure enough, sheets of rain swept across Thunder Egg Downs.

Charlie realized that the story was going on without him. Sooner or later, he would have to make a decision—be rid of his half of the book or fully embrace the story. The afternoon bell rang and the children left for the day. Charlie sat in the classroom, waiting, looking out the window as the driving rain continued. He felt so alone. No one cared. He was in this all by himself. Then a voice disturbed his teary state.

"Is our birthday boy coming home for his birthday feast?" Sylvia Ramsbottom was standing behind Charlie, Cecil by her side. Charlie turned to his parents and hugged them.

As the Ramsbottoms drove home, the storm grew wilder. The rain lashed and buffeted the car and blew the wipers off the windscreen. Inwardly, Charlie became very still. Moving closer to his parents, he spoke quietly and resolutely, "This storm is my fault. You know, I could stop this if I wanted to."

Charlie's parents just looked at the road ahead and agreed, like parents do when their children make up wonderfully imaginative stories.

"No, really! I could. I could stop this storm if I wanted to. It's just that I'm...I'm scared of what will happen if I do." Mr. Ramsbottom pulled the car over to the side of the road.

"Charlie, this is your decision. If you want to end the storm and rescue the eagles, then it's up to you. We won't stand in your way. It's your choice. Do you think you're up to it?"

Charlie was speechless.

"Cecil, I think we'd better get home," said Mrs. Ramsbottom with quiet authority. "Charlie can make his decision over a nice hot bowl of hard-boiled eggplant curry."

"What's going on? How do you know about this?" demanded Charlie. Charlie's parents turned to him.

They spoke in unison. "Bizz-Buzz!" Charlie's father released the car's hand-break and they drove off towards Thunder Egg Farm, traversing huge pools of water that were flooding the road. When they arrived at the farmhouse, Charlie was shocked. The rain was destroying fences and crops. Torrents of water were gradually filling up the River Googly that ran close to the chicken coop. Snoozeball, Runningmouth and the rest of the chickens were soaked to the skin, drenched as they tried to divert the rising water away from their prized dwelling. At the rate the river was flowing, the chicken coop would be under water in an hour.

All of a sudden, a deafening roar permeated the landscape. The Ramsbottoms looked at each other not knowing what the noise was. Jumping out of the car, they ran to a vantage point on top of the hill where they saw a wall of water, a veritable tsunami racing towards their farmhouse, wrecking everything in its path. And directly in the way of the huge wave was Penelope, obliviously walking towards the house, screeching out another Mozartian aria, with her headphones dangling precariously from her ears, her red hair plastered to her head. Charlie hated his sister's guts, but not enough to watch her die.

"This must be Skunk Weavel's work," said Charlie, knowing that he would have to act quickly. He raced back to the car, grabbed *The Book* and laid it open on the hood. With the rain soaking him through to the skin, he raised his arms to the sky and shouted to the wind.

"I don't know who you are, Bizz-Buzz, but tell Moon I'm ready to save his family. Please stop the rain, RIGHT NOW!"

The rain ceased, and like a breath caught before its release, the wave paused at Charlie's command and then retreated from whence it had come, completely disappearing from sight. Penelope was utterly unaware of the wave and how close she had been to death. She made her way into the house and up to her room. As she climbed the steps to the house, the thunderclouds parted and the sun broke through, sending a ray of light down onto Charlie who looked up as he heard an awkward flapping sound. From out of the sun, he saw Moon flying towards him very fast. Before he could move out of the way, Moon hit the roof of the car, skidded across the shiny metallic surface and fell into Charlie's arms.

"It's about time you made a decision. That was a close call," squawked Moon. "I've been swirling around, trapped in those thunder clouds for what seemed like a lifetime, waiting for you to make up your mind."

"I think we'd better all go inside and eat your birthday feast while we make an urgent plan to rescue Moon's family. If the eagles aren't saved, then…" said Mrs. Ramsbottom not daring to finish her thought. When they went inside the house, the delightful smell of hard-boiled eggplant curry flooded their nostrils. They were all so ravenous that they devoured the food in no time at all. (Except for Penelope, who was in her room, busily solving algebraic equations, or so they thought.) No one spoke during the meal, for they knew that what lay ahead for Charlie would indeed be dangerous.

Once the meal was finished, Mr. Ramsbottom pulled out a map of Thunder Egg Farm and its surroundings and showed Charlie and Moon the route they should take to leave the Shire of Tumblegum. Giving her husband a nod, Mrs. Ramsbottom slipped discreetly out of the door to go and get Charlie's real birthday present. While she was gone, Mr. Ramsbottom told Charlie about Bizz-Buzz. Charlie listened closely.

"When I found the Thunder Eggs that day out on the lake, Charlie, something else happened. As soon as they were in my boat, everything seemed to stop. I turned around and there, standing on the water, was a man wearing a long greatcoat and snow-colored gloves. He told me his name was Bizz-Buzz. I was petrified at first, but he was very friendly. He bizzed and he buzzed and told me that a huge web connects us all, and if I could save these enormously special eggs, it would help us make the farm work. We were extremely poor at the time and there was something unbelievably believable about him. I just couldn't refuse. Then he disappeared." Charlie sat very still.

His father continued, "Last night, Bizz-Buzz paid us another visit and said to give you the book and that one day you would understand." Mr. Ramsbottom was starting to become emotional but Charlie remained quiet. His skin was starting to itch again!

From outside, Sylvia Ramsbottom called urgently to them. Charlie, Moon and Mr. Ramsbottom ran to see what the fuss was. Sylvia was standing next to an oversized extra-long skateboard. "Wicked!! It's exactly the same as the one in *The Book of Dreams*," gasped Charlie.

"When the wind rises upon the Plains of Desire, you must pull on this sail Charlie," she said pointing to a small lever attached to the board. "It'll drive you faster across the Plains and help to protect you. Now, we have to go to the chicken coop and get our special eggs. I think two is all you can fit on your new board." Hurriedly, they all made their way to the chicken coop and down to the dormitory.

Inside the coop, most of the chickens were drying off while finishing their afternoon tea. Sitting at the long table playing Happy Families were Snoozeball and Runningmouth. Surrounded by hot chocolate and rice pudding, they greeted Charlie, Moon and the Ramsbottoms, like old friends, then led them to an area marked "Fresh Eggs." Two eggs rumbled down the chute and sploshed into the water.

"There you go, there you go, there you go," said a bedraggled Runningmouth. "Two wonderful, mouth watering, palate captivating eggs. I hope you are not going to put them all in one basket because...."

"Here are your eggs," interrupted Snoozeball. Mr. and Mrs. Ramsbottom each picked up one of the large, heavy Thunder Eggs and held them carefully in their arms. They were still warm. The party went upstairs where they placed the eggs carefully on the skateboard before securing them with rope and canvas.

Very soon, it was time to leave. Charlie kissed and hugged his mother and father goodbye. A wind started blowing through the trees suggesting that another storm was approaching. Charlie's father shouted through the wind to his son, "When you return, we'll have the biggest birthday party that anyone has ever seen in Thunder Egg Downs!"

Suddenly, two pairs of dark wings emerged from the clouds. Snarlies!

"*The Book*!" said Charlie. "And your other present," said Mr. Ramsbottom. They both rushed into the house climbing the stairs two at a time. Charlie retrieved the book and slid it into his schoolbag. His father picked up the conch and gave it to Charlie who placed it next to the book. Quickly, Mr. Ramsbottom ran back outside to tie the canvas down even tighter. From the doorway, Charlie took one last nostalgic look around his bedroom. Would he ever come back? As he was going down the stairs, Penelope opened her door very slightly and glared at her brother. She was chewing on a stringy piece of gooba, like it was licorice.

"I'm ready for you, Creep," she whispered to herself, out of Charlie's earshot. "I'll be waiting for you when you least expect it."

When Charlie returned outside, the wind was becoming stronger and stronger. A gaggle of chickens, led by Snoozeball and Runningmouth, had come to bid them good luck and farewell.

"Go to the forest, laddie," shouted Charlie's father. "It'll protect you from the storm until you reach the edge of town. Then you must travel across the Plains of Desire. They will lead you to the city...to the city..." Mr. Ramsbottom couldn't say the words he was so frightened of their power.

"What did you say, Dad? I can't hear you!" Charlie shouted, the approaching winds becoming more ferocious. A trembling Mr. Ramsbottom replied,

"Take the Plains of Desire to the City...the City...the City of the Quincequonces," he shouted, worry racking his face. Then he blurted out, "Charlie. I love you!" Very quickly he added, "Read the instructions on the conch before you use it. It's from Bizz-Buzz." Mr. Ramsbottom turned away and blew his nose with a great honk.

"Yes, that's right, that's quite right. I couldn't agree more, absolutely..." said Runningmouth. She was about to ramble on when Snoozeball clamped her claw across her friend's mouth, just as an awful noise started to fill the air. They all looked to the sky. Flip and Flop were closing in.

The screeching, arguing clatter of the two Snarlies grew in intensity, accompanied by huge fists of lightning ripping across Thunder Egg Downs. There were plenty of hugs and rivers of tears as they parted. Waving goodbye, Charlie loaded the little eagle onto the skateboard and pushed it so it sped off towards the forest. The journey to save Moon's family and *The Book of Dreams* had finally begun!

END OF PART ONE

PART TWO: THE WAY OF RAMSBOTTOM

Chapter Eight: The Water Test

Charlie and Moon had just passed into the cover of Tumblegum Forest when the Snarlies began dive-bombing Thunder Egg Farm. You could hear the gooba gurgling in their snouts as the two gruesome hulks of feather and leather broke through a bank of blustery clouds at slime-speed, growling, snapping and screwing up their faces in threatening gestures.

Catching a last look back through a gap in the trees, Charlie watched his father fight through a powerful gust of wind to help his mother mount the steps of their home. Sylvia turned to gaze in the direction in which Charlie had entered the forest. She gave Cecil a kiss on the cheek and a reassuring hug before they disappeared into the farmhouse.

Watching the love between his parents, Charlie felt a lump in his throat, but this soon dissolved like sugar in tea as the two Snarlies crash-landed. Dusting themselves off, they adjusted their night-vision goggles and headed straight towards the forest. But the loyal, wily Thunder Egg chickens had a plan. When

Snoozeball pulled out a pack of cards—a pack of Happy Families —she stopped the Snarlies in their tracks.

Bursting into laughter, Flip shouted cockily above the roar of the wind, "So, you want a re-match, do ya pardner?"

Runningmouth, who wasn't about to be undone by Flip's bravado, returned the Snarlies' call confidently, although her knees still shook in the evil bird's presence.

"Well, how dare you," she replied, giving Flop a welcoming look that said, *I'm mighty pleased to see you again, baby!*

"How dare you come back here," she continued, "and challenge my, my, my friend and me to a re-match of Happy Families when you completely, totally, utterly fooled us last time and thrashed us. As if you didn't know," she said with a twinkle in her eye, "You two Snarlies are the finest players of Happy Families that we've come across anywhere in the whole world and..." Snoozeball tapped her friend on the wing as if to say, "don't overdo it, dear."

"If you gentlemen would consider the following suggestion," Snoozeball said elegantly. The Snarlies adjusted their day-night goggles and stared at her suspiciously as she reeled out the bait. "The table downstairs is set for four players. The mugs of chocolate are piping hot. The rice pudding is bubbling—almost ready. All we have to do is add the double clotted cream and fresh homemade strawberry jam." A trickle of light green gooba ran down Flip's cheek and Flop's stomach churgled in anticipation of good food and some time with his chicky-baby. And, their master hadn't fed them anything but dried cornflakes and rancid rainwater for the past few weeks.

"Would you like to follow us?" Snoozeball queried as Flop wiped a trickle from his snout. For a while, there was a general to-ing and fro-ing with some give and take until the heavens opened. Then, to avert the rain, the four birds quickly negotiated a truce.

Watching the feathered quartet rush down to the chicken dormitory was how Charlie remembered leaving Thunder Egg Farm. He knew that the Snarlies had been diverted from their goal, if only temporarily. Immediately, he turned his attention to the task at hand—the journey through the forest.

After the storm, the forest had become a confusing mass of creepy crawlies, strange shadowy specters and soaring canopies that shut out the sky. As Charlie pushed the skateboard along the forest's sticky pathways, Moon could see that his young friend was struggling, so he jumped onto his shoulder and nestled into the side of Charlie's neck to give him some comfort and keep a watch-out for the enemy. Both of them knew inwardly that what lay ahead would indeed be difficult, unpredictable and extremely dangerous. And each knew that he dared not tell the other how terrified he was.

Within the first half hour of the expedition, they had to take many detours, hardly making any headway. Great splintered shafts of tree trunks and huge, enormous fallen branches, like the legs of the most gargantuan goblins, obstructed their path. Charlie found that pushing the skateboard was incredibly hard and tiring. The weight of the two Thunder Eggs and the extremely muddy tracks made the early part of the journey painfully slow and arduous. Sometimes there was no track at all. In fact, it felt to Charlie like they were riding on a mass of wriggling worms, which almost drove him to madness.

Worst of all was the intrusiveness of the rain as it found its way into every nook and cranny of Charlie's being. Waterlogged shoes, drenched clothing, dripping hair; Charlie felt like a cold hot-water bottle, squishing and squashing along the almost invisible pathway. At one point, he sensed that someone or something was following them. A freezing wet shiver ran down his spine. His head whipped around, but before he could stop to see who or what the danger might be, an enticing voice began whispering in his ear. Slowly coiling around his mind, like a python squeezing the life out of a stick of rhubarb, the voice hissed the following advice:

"Listen carefully, Charlie Ramsbottom. You'll get nowhere with that loser of a bird. Just give him up. As your good friend, it's my job to tell you, you're wasting your time. Give him up. He's a waster. That's right, my little friend, a waster. Leave him and the book to me, and you can have anything you like—Game Boys, X-Boxes, Nintendo, the latest EM9—you name it, it's yours. I promise to make you the most powerful boy in the world: the most powerful boy. It's in your best interest. Think about it."

Charlie did think about it and it made him so scared that his legs shook like jelly wobbles. He recognized the voice. He knew who it was. It was the voice of Skunk Weavel. The same voice who had called the Snarlie's back to The City of The Quincequonces on the two-way radio. The voice from *The Book*.

"Whatever you imagine, will you become, Charlie," hissed the toymaker. *"All the power will be yours."*

"Leave me alone, leave alone," muttered Charlie to himself.

"When you are king, you'll be able to do and have anything!"

"What do you mean—anything?" asked Charlie secretively. "Do you actually mean *anything*?"

"A-n-y-t-h-i-n-g and e-v-e-r-y-t-h-i-n-g," replied the toymaker, deep into Charlie's soul. Charlie was edging towards a huge fall from grace when Moon squawked out aloud. He jumped down from Charlie's shoulder onto the skateboard and began to sing a song to the tune of "Dixie":

"We're going on a journey to save my clan
10,000 eagle hops to stop a naughty man,
To stop, to stop, a very naughty man.
I'm proud to be an eagle, that's bold and true.
A Blue and Gold Winged eagle
that's coming after you,
Sku – hunk Weavel, I'm coming after you."

When Moon finished his song, he laughed out loud but Charlie was too busy to hear him. He was battling the weather on a number of fronts. The ferocious wind was shrieking with laughter at him. The constant hammering of the rain was pounding in his brain like a jackhammer. The noise was absolutely unbearable. Even more disconcerting were the continuing reminders in his inner ear from the evil Weavel that Moon was a waster and Charlie could be all powerful. The toymaker would not give up.

"Why would you want to hang out with such an arrogant

bird?" whispered the toymaker into Charlie's ear. *"He's just a useless good-for-nothing and you could be so powerful if you erased him from the picture."*

Charlie looked at Moon as the bird pranced up and down. Skunk continued weavelling his spell around Charlie.

"All he does is complain. You'll get tired of that, Charlie. I can offer you a lot more. I can offer you the world."

Charlie pressed onwards, but he was rapidly losing his grip of the ultimate goal. After a few hundred more mucky steps, the two came to a clearing that looked as if it had been ripped out of the earth by the hands of an angry giant. Charlie pulled out a map from his schoolbag and tried to read it in the forest's fading light.

"Hurry up, Ramsbottom. Do hurry!" shouted an anxious Moon. "I want to get at that toymaker as soon as I can and we haven't got much time left." In the diminishing light, Charlie tried to make sense of the map, but as this was the first time that he'd read any map at all, the details just looked like lines and squiggles and meant absolutely nothing to him. To add to Charlie's confusion, the wind and the rain attacked each other like a pack of wild dogs.

Amidst this chaos, there suddenly came a lull and an eerie silence. They were at Thunder Egg Bridge. Charlie remembered how he had been there many times before with his mother, identifying over two hundred species of butterflies on pleasant spring afternoons, when he hadn't a worry in the world. Now, through the stillness, only the crashing sound of water could be heard. It sounded like rapids. Charlie walked over to the edge of the bridge and looked down. Peering through the mist, he could see torrents of water smashing about on the rocks below. He took another step forward. There was a sharp cracking and splintering of wood. Then there was only air under his feet. For the briefest of moments he started to fly—downwards. Just as quickly, he felt his body jerk in mid-air. His stomach rushed up to his mouth and back again. A revolting taste filled his throat. Right at that moment, the rain stopped to reveal that the one hundred-year-old slatted, wooden bridge had been snapped in half under the pressure of a fallen oak. Charlie was hanging in space only because his bag had jagged a piece of the broken oak. He looked up but couldn't see Moon.

"Help! Moon! Please help me. Quick!" Charlie screamed but Moon was nowhere to be seen as the river reached up, licking at his feet.

"Moon! Where are you?" yelled Charlie. Still no response! The toymaker had been right. Moon was completely useless. Charlie was starting to get very cold and could feel his body stiffening. The river was raging below him, almost calling him to let go. He grabbed one of the broken wooden slats and its needle-like slivers splintered his hand. This time, his scream was one of sheer pain but still there was no response from the little eagle.

Gritting his teeth, he started to agonizingly pull himself up the rope of wood, inch by inch. Sweat poured down his face. The feeling in his throat told him he was right on the verge of puking. And he was absolutely terrified of falling to his death. It could be his last moment on earth and he was only nine! There was so much to do and it just wasn't fair! When he had almost reached safety, he slipped again. Free falling for a split second, he grabbed another piece of the bridge as he was about to plunge into oblivion. His arms felt like they were being wrenched from out of their sockets. Slowly but surely with his body drenched in the most disgusting smelling sweat, he heaved himself up until he lay horizontal on the broken slats, sobs racking his body. He was shaking and mumbling uncontrollably.

"What are you doing? Where have you been? Get up! We can't waste any more time. Let's get going," shouted Moon. Charlie shakily stood up, dumbstruck and exasperated that Moon had no idea of what had just occurred. However, Moon *had* been looking furiously for Charlie but Charlie had just disappeared from sight and the roar of the rapids had obliterated his cries for help.

Still shivering, Charlie took a deep breath.

"What are we going to do? We can't cross the bridge," said Charlie

"Well, we'll have to find another way," said Moon. "We have to move quickly to save my family."

"Don't you think I *know* that?" retorted Charlie, thinking that Moon was stating the obvious.

"Don't get shirty with me," shouted Moon.

"You could come up with a suggestion," Charlie shouted back.

"Have a look in the book," replied Moon. "The book is sure to know." The fact that it was so obvious to the eagle annoyed Charlie because he had not thought of it. From his bag, he pulled out the book and tried to open it but the pages wouldn't budge. No matter how hard he tried to lever the pages open, the book remained tightly shut. Finally, he wedged it against the edge of the skateboard and with every ounce of strength that he could muster, yanked the jeweled cover open. An enormous flash of fire burst out of the book and the pages fluttered madly about in the wind. Feeling nervous, Charlie held the ancient book open to the last glimmer of light struggling through the canopy. He stood statue-like and his face turned an ashen grey.

"What's the matter? What's the matter?" called Moon. Reluctantly, Charlie showed Moon the book. On the page, flashing in blood red neon with a picture of the two Snarlies laughing, were the following words:

**Do not open the book in the forest.
If you do, the Snarlies will immediately
know where you are!**

As he slammed the book shut, green gooba seeped out from the pages. Charlie quickly tucked the book securely into his bag and zipped it up. Instantly, the approaching whine of the Snarlies could be heard. The second game of Happy Families was over. Flip and Flop were searching for them.

"Oh, no! I've done it this time," moaned Charlie.

"Stop wasting time! Let's cross the bridge," shouted Moon.

"No. Don't you see, we can't," said Charlie.

"Let me have a look at those pages again," demanded Moon as Charlie felt his arms tighten around the bag.

"No. No. No. I am the keeper of this book," Charlie said adamantly, hardly believing what was coming from his lips. It was like another voice was speaking through him. Moon looked at him suspiciously while Charlie continued as if in a daze.

"I don't know why, but the book's spirit tried to protect me...tried to stop me from opening the cover but I went against it. Now our only chance is...the river. Yes, the river." Even as the words crossed his lips, Charlie had already begun sliding the skateboard down the muddy slope straight towards the water. The argumentative wheezing commotion of the Snarlies drew closer.

"Are you crazy?" screamed Moon, thinking Charlie was going to push the board into the water. "We'll never survive these rapids. This is mad. Yes, you're mad. We'll never survive." Moon continued to yell at the top of his voice but Charlie was too busy to pay attention to the eagle. Maneuvering the skateboard along the edges of the riverbank, he desperately tried to keep his feet from slipping and, at the same time, was ever mindful of the foaming water raging right next to them.

Then it happened. In the blink of an eye, Charlie lost his footing, then his grip and before you could say "Skunk Weavel," the board, with Moon on it had slipped into the river and both were gliding away from Charlie through a wall of black water. Moon tried to spread his tiny wings around the Thunder Eggs and cried out for Charlie to save him but the only sound Charlie could hear was the crashing of the rapids all around.

Soaked to the skin, Charlie darted along the rain-sodden bank trying to follow the skateboard's course but it was impossible. A broken limb of a tree bobbed into view and Charlie was onto it in a flash. He dived into the water without any fear and grabbed onto the branch. That was when it came to him: with the frenzied rapids beginning to take him on a wild and out-of-control ride, he had a very interesting insight—he remembered he couldn't swim. Fear overtaking him, he gripped the branch like a vice with one hand while the other held the bag close to his body. Mr. Grumblebum's lesson on how to stay afloat in a raging river suddenly took on a whole new meaning. Furiously, the surging water pulled him sideways, up and down, over and under, round and about like a rag-doll being spun by a crazed washing machine.

For the briefest of moments, there seemed to be a relief from the floodwater. Spitting out what seemed like a lung-full of muddy slime; Charlie gasped and sucked in the air, trying to regain his strength. He was utterly exhausted. Then rounding a bend in the river, he chanced to look up and let out an enormous cry; heading straight towards him was a huge wave that intended to smash him to smithereens. It was too late to do anything except surrender to his fear. The wave dragged him unceremoniously right into the center, tossing and throwing him about viciously. He could see virtually nothing, which was probably just as well, for he would have died of shock with all the near misses he had.

Fighting for his life, Charlie became acutely aware of the one thing that could possibly save him—the piece of advice his teacher had given that very morning. It came to him clear as crystal, "…when you're in a tight situation, relax." He could almost hear Mr. Grumblebum's thick Indian accent uttering these sensible words. Remembering the instruction, Charlie dropped slowly backwards into the foaming rapids and closed his eyes. In an instant, loving thoughts of his mother and father flashed before him. Pictures whizzed across his inner screen of Moon and how the story had unfolded. Even fond memories of Penelope seeped into his brain.

On every side, trees crashed down, smashing into thousands of pieces, ripped by the jagged rocks that lined the riverbanks. The wind whipped up the river with the force of a hurricane and the waves crashed high over Charlie's head. But Charlie was in another world, imagining his favorite dinner—home-made baked beans, fries, two eggs, sunny side up and thick slices of whole-wheat toast, smeared with butter and creamed honey. Charlie was having such a good time making sure that the beans were cooked to his satisfaction, he didn't even realize that he was being flipped up high into the air by another huge wave and thrown towards a set of jagged rocks that would spell his end forever. In fact, he was so relaxed, he didn't even see the white-bearded man and the woman with the beehive hairdo holding out their arms to catch him, and then lay him down gently on the river's edge under some trees. It felt just like his mother putting him to bed on the softest of sheets.

Charlie clung to the bank, completely worn out. Quite near to him was the skateboard, resting against a battered tree trunk with the eggs surprisingly secure. He was about to stand up and search for Moon, when a new threat became obvious–the sound of Flip and Flop patrolling the embankment right in front of him, discussing the second card game. Drawing nearer, the stench from the Snarlies became worse and worse until it was almost impossible to take. Clearly, the two uglies had avoided cleaning their beaks for weeks. (And you could bet they didn't floss them either.) Charlie lay there with the fingers of one hand crossed, praying that he wouldn't be seen or smelled. With the fingers of his other hand, he pinched his nose to ward off the pungent odor. From the sound of Flip's agitated conversation with his partner, the second round of Happy Families had not gone well; they had lost to the Thunder Egg Chickens. Flip was seriously annoyed.

"How embarrassing! How humiliating! I bet those crafty, sneaky, sniveling chickens drugged the hot chocolate or the rice pudding or both," snarled Flip. "They must have drugged yours at least Flop, because you acted so stupidly and played like an ant with half a brain. Mrs. Bun the Baker and Mr. Plod the Policeman! How many times have I told you? You need a pair. A pair! It's a game. It's not real life. They don't have to get married. They don't want to get married. They don't even know each other. What's more, I bet they don't even like each other. So, in future, just lay down pairs." Flip was fuming. "Now the scores are level, and you can bet your bottom dollar they'll want revenge. Well, next time, we'll trick 'em." Flip laughed at his own suggestion, Flop echoed in response, too afraid of his brother-at-arms not to.

As if Charlie's prayers had been heard, the Snarlies moved away. Feeling brave again, Charlie checked that everything was in order. The Thunder Eggs were still safe. The skateboard was in pretty good shape considering the battering it had taken. But Moon: he was nowhere to be seen. Where was he? Charlie began to walk up and down, cursing himself like a madman.

"You idiot! What are you going to do now? They'll say you killed him....Oh, please Moon, where are you, where are you?" Once more, the evil voice of Skunk Weavel began to envelop him.

"You have done my work for me, Charlie Ramsbottom. Forget the bird now. He's gone. Bring the book to me. The story is over. It's time for you to become the numero uno boy in the world, the numero uno boy."

Charlie toyed with Skunk's suggestion even more now and as he did, the inner door of his mind creaked open. It was enough to allow the evil spirit of the toymaker to enter Charlie's thoughts like a cockroach foraging for food in a dark corner. At once, the promises of power increased and became more real. Charlie saw himself wearing a crown. He was going to become a king. Yes. A king, and he would be able to have and do anything. He'd be able to drink all the fizzy drinks he wanted, eat all the cream buns in the world, have all the latest video games, never have to go to school, hang out with his friends all the time and take them for drives in one of his latest sports cars, because as king he'd be given a special driving licence that would give him the power to drive without having to learn. He was the king, and he could do anything he liked. Amidst this regal reverie, another voice called to him, a familiar lilting voice that cut through the night.

"Stop! Stay where you are! Don't move!" Charlie stood absolutely motionless, landing back in reality. "So easy to find, Charlie Ramsbottom. So easy to find," whispered the voice. Charlie held his breath. He could see the vague outline of a figure, a figure wearing what looked like a balaclava, waddling towards him very slowly, making a strange splish-sploshing sound. The figure was closer now. It was also wearing underwater goggles, a wet suit and a small oxygen tank on its back. It breathed heavily into Charlie's face. A flashlight clicked on, momentarily blinding him. Then a cold vice-like hand gripped Charlie's wrist.

"That's the idiot who tried to kill me," squawked a high-pitched voice, coughing up water all over Charlie's face. "That's him."

Chapter Nine: Unknown Allies

The unknown entity pulled the goggles from its face. There stood Mr. Grumblebum, Charlie's teacher, wearing a complete frogman's outfit. Moon was perched on his shoulder, looking distraught and very bedraggled.

"Next time you decide to risk my life, Ramsbottom," shouted the furious eagle, "would you at least give me more than five seconds warning!" Turning his head away in utter disgust, he coughed up more river water.

"Mr. Grumblebum! What are you doing here? And Moon. How did you find him?" gasped Charlie, the glare from the torch momentarily lighting up his teacher's face like a ghoul. While Moon continued to spit out the last remnants of the river from his tiny body, Mr. Grumblebum peered into the night and spoke like a man possessed.

"If you're going to fulfill your mission, Charlie Ramsbottom...," he said in his lilting accent, "...you're going to have to be a lot smarter than you were at those rapids."

For one unwavering moment, the teacher and boy stared intensely at each other. Charlie was about to ask Mr. Grumblebum what he meant, when *bing!* the teacher's eyes flashed like car headlights, startling Charlie. "Quick, you'd better come with me. We'll have to disguise you, otherwise you won't be able to give those Snarlies the slip."

The teacher set off slowly, splish-sploshing like a duck. Very soon, they reached the back streets of Thunder Egg Downs village. Passing the buildings, Charlie recalled that the unusual town was made of the strongest toasted bread in case of a repeat of the famine, which had raged nine years earlier, just before Charlie was born. If the famine ever came again, at least the villagers could eat the buildings to survive.

Charlie followed Mr. Grumblebum, pushing the skateboard up a steady incline with Moon sitting astride the Thunder Eggs. The group passed a cluster of shops. In a flash, Mr. Grumblebum pulled them into the shadowy doorway of Smellie's Bakery. At the rear of the bakery, Mrs. Smellie could be seen making another batch of her famous fruit loaves. Charlie's stomach grumbled so loudly that he almost didn't hear a wheezing sound approaching. It was Snarlie bird Flop in search of Moon. The unsightly bird was only about one eagle hop from Charlie, Moon and Mr. Grumblebum when he stopped and started talking to himself.

"Now if Flip plays Mr. Plod the Policeman, surely I could play Mrs. Bun the Baker because I think she and the policeman like each other and they would make a lovely pair. Whereas, Flip says I should play Mrs. Plod the Policewoman and then that would be a pair. But I'm not sure if they even like each other. I suppose Flip's got his reasons but I reckon Mrs.Bun the Baker and Mr. Plod the Policeman would make a much better match because they've got such a lot in common—she makes cakes and he likes to eat them." Flop was pleased now that he'd brilliantly worked out *his* interpretation of Happy Families." He moved away from the three figures hiding in the shadows. Mr. Grumblebum tugged on Charlie's hand.

"Where are we going?" inquired Charlie, while Mr. Grumblebum slid along the edges of buildings, making sure the toast was clear.

"We're going to a friend's house. She's been waiting for us; waiting *ever* since you left Thunder Egg Farm."

"But who, who is she? What's happening?" asked a confused Charlie of his teacher who had waddled around a corner towards a quaint fruit-loaf cottage, where the lights were burning brightly.

"Stay here while I check to make sure it's safe," whispered Mr. Grumblebum. He crawled into the garden, peered through the windows and then called *pssst*, beckoning Charlie and Moon towards the cottage. Charlie parked the skateboard and Thunder Eggs next to the gate, and carefully lifted Moon into his arms. They crossed the lawn to where Mr. Grumblebum waited anxiously for them on the porch. Silently, the teacher led the boy and the bird inside the small dwelling and closed the door.

Once inside, Charlie gazed around the tiny candle-lit cottage, which was cramped beyond description. Against three of the room's fruit bread plastered walls were books of all colors and sizes, stacked and piled high to the ceiling. Near to the other wall, facing a roaring fire stood a woman wearing a patchwork dressing gown. As she turned to face them, Moon squawked at the woman's ghastly appearance. She had rollers in her hair and an organic wheat germ and seaweed cream mask, plastered across her face. When she smiled at them (and the whole world smiled when she did) her teeth took on a mustardy yellow tinge. Charlie's jaw dropped in disbelief. It was the school librarian, Noni Benoni. Noni took Mr. Grumblebum's hand in hers when she saw Charlie and Moon.

"Oh, thank God you found them, Eric. Thank God!" she said. Mr. Eric Grumblebum smiled in embarrassment.

"Too easy to find if you ask me. Too easy to find. They're safe, but not for long. We'll have to disguise them; otherwise they won't even get out of the village. The Snarlies are patrolling the streets."

Although he was only nine, Charlie sensed that there was something more than just a teacher-librarian association between Ms. Benoni and Mr. Grumblebum. They were obviously related—perhaps brother and sister. Whatever it was, Charlie was utterly amazed at seeing them together out of class. And now they were in cahoots. Wait until he told everyone at school. Wouldn't they all be shocked, especially Penelope and her know-it-all friends.

Noni turned to Charlie, gave him a hot cup of tea and whispered, "Well Charlie, aren't you going to formally introduce us?" Charlie felt a little silly introducing a bird to people.

"Ms. Benoni, Mr. Grumblebum. This is Moon. He is a Royal Blue-and-Gold-winged eagle whose entire family are prisoners of Skunk Weavel." Moon bowed and squawked in Eaglish that he was pleased to meet them and thanked them for their help.

Once Charlie had translated, Noni Benoni cleared her throat and spoke, "We are honored to meet you Moon, but time is short and we need to find a way of disguising you and Charlie so that you can make it safely to the City of the Quincequonces."

"How are you two involved in all of this?" asked Charlie. Mr. Grumblebum and Noni Benoni replied in unison.

"Bizz-Buzz," they said. Noni went on. "When we heard your tale at school today, we knew that the time had come for you to undertake your mission. We had to pretend that we didn't believe your story Charlie, because we are sworn to secrecy by Bizz-Buzz. However, we are allowed to help you on the journey, in any way we can."

"But why me?" implored Charlie. "Why?" Mr. Grumblebum put his arm around Charlie and drew him near to the fire. Charlie's wet clothes started to steam.

"All that I can tell you Charlie, is that whoever has *The Book of Dreams* protects or controls our dreams and desires. You have half and Skunk Weavel has half and therein lies the problem. For some reason, you were chosen by Bizz-Buzz to be the keeper of this half of *The Book*. And you are the only one who can stop Weavel because of your ability to communicate with both animals and humans and…," he added quietly, "…because of your gift."

"Bizz-Buzz? Talk to the animals? Gift? What gift?" demanded Charlie.

His mouth started to become dry. His palms started to itch. Mr. Grumblebum continued, "Today is a special day, the day of threes. It's your ninth birthday and it's the longest day of the year on this side of the world and the shortest day on the other. It is the time when the planets line up with their equivalent constellations and the only day of the year when *The Book of Dreams* can be reunited. You must wrest the other half of the book from Skunk Weavel and join the two together. However, if Skunk gets his hands on *your* half of *The Book*, he will take control of all of our dreams and the universe will no longer be in harmony!"

Charlie drew in a long breath and was just about to try and get a word in edgewise when Mr. Grumblebum drew an even longer breath. He was on a roll.

"Beware my young friend, because you will be tempted. You probably already have been." Charlie thought of Skunk Weavel's taunts and shuffled his feet awkwardly. His skin started to itch most annoyingly. Mr. Grumblebum motioned for Charlie to come closer.

"Unite *The Book* and return those eagles to their rightful place by the time the clock strikes midnight."

"How'd you know about Bizz-Buzz? What did he tell you? And why aren't you telling me?"

Ignoring Charlie's questions, Mr. Grumblebum began mixing a special liquid concoction.

"Some things are best left unsaid," said Noni. "Sometimes it's better to find out things as they happen. If you knew before the event what was going to happen, perhaps you might not want to go."

"Oh, yeah, like that makes me feel really safe," replied Charlie. "Now all I want to do is go back home and climb into bed and forget all of this!" Noni looked at Charlie and then at his teacher. Charlie saw the look.

"Come on. You know something. What are you not telling me?"

Noni hushed him and told him to change his clothes. From out of her collection of school play costumes piled high in one corner of the room, she found a pirate's outfit, replete with eye patch. While he changed his clothes, Charlie checked to see if the contents of his bag were waterlogged. Thankfully, the book was dry. He picked up the conch that his father had given him and read the engraving on it.

This conch can only be used twice.
Once for an extreme emergency and...
a second time for a really, really
extreme emergency.
Signed: Bizz-Buzz

When Charlie placed the conch back in the bag, he saw his teacher watching him. Mr. Grumblebum averted his gaze and pretended to finish making the concoction. Noni stole a nervous glance at Charlie then peered back at Eric Grumblebum. Immediately, they said, "The Conch of the Great Ocean—it's worse than we thought. We haven't much time." Charlie went to speak but Noni put her finger to his lips and carefully looked around her.

"We don't know who is listening, who's a friend and who's not," she said cautiously. "The land, the actual land itself is on the verge of something awful and we must be extremely careful.

Dangerous times are afoot." Charlie remained very quiet. Noni continued, her voice wavering. "Just yesterday, Skunk Weavel captured…" She couldn't go on, she was so upset. Mr. Grumblebum put his arm around her and took up the story, but his voice was also shaky. "Late yesterday, that awful toymaker sent his Snarlies to trap the last remaining tribe of Teddy Bears, the lost tribe led by Sir Edward Bainbridge." Charlie groaned aloud when he heard this. How could someone take out the last tribe of Teddy Bears—they were almost extinct —it would mean the end of their time on the planet. Now, more than ever before, everything seemed to rest upon Charlie saving Moon's family and defeating the rapacious toymaker. Which animals would the toymaker wipe out next if Charlie didn't stop him?

Noni hurriedly dressed Moon in a parrot's outfit, so he could sit on Charlie's shoulder and shout out things like, "Pieces of eight, pieces of eight." Charlie sat in the corner drinking his tea, thinking to himself and staring at Moon. The others didn't know it, but Skunk Weavel was whispering in his ear again.

"Put the bird in the rubbish bin. He's a loser. You will be king. King! My numero uno boy. Or would you rather that pathetic eagle be king instead?" Charlie was completely perplexed and out of sorts, not knowing what to do when Moon began complaining about his own disguise.

"I'm not too sure I like being a parrot," said Moon. "I mean, I'm a royal eagle, not a parrot. I'm heir to the throne."

When Charlie told the others what Moon had said, they all stood still, and stopped what they were doing. There and then, they realized that they were dealing with the next king of the eagles. This was serious business. That's why Moon was sent to find Charlie. A task fit only for a king. No wonder the Snarlie's were so keen to catch him. Charlie became just a smidge-bit jealous of Moon.

"The only other outfit I've got is a prawn costume...that would be far too silly," said Noni, changing the subject. "Besides, you look very handsome as a parrot, Moon...sire." The little prince fluttered his wings and looked in a mirror opposite the door. Yes, he did look handsome.

It was time to leave. Mr. Grumblebum went outside to stabilize the skateboard, tighten the ropes and secure the eggs while Noni finished preparing some food and drink for the journey. She picked some rose chocolates from off a climbing bush just outside her window and filled a thermos flask with the concoction that Mr. Grumblebum had been working on. Charlie put the chocolates and the thermos into his bag and was just closing it when Mr. Grumblebum came dashing back into the house looking terribly distressed.

"What's wrong Eric, what's wrong?" cried Noni.

"The skateboard! The eggs! They're gone. GONE!" They all ran outside, Moon bouncing on Charlie's shoulder. What Mr. Grumblebum had said was true. The skateboard and the eggs had disappeared.

Frustrated, Charlie started to cry. All his hard work was lost—disappeared, just like that. They would have to go back and start all over again.

"Don't whine, Charlie. You've got to think of something," said Moon, obviously concerned that his protector and fellow adventurer was turning into a crybaby. "You're a pirate now and pirates don't cry. They...do something. Understand? D-O! DO!"

"O.K. Moon. O.K. I get the message!" sniffled Charlie, showing the first signs of annoyance at Moon's attitude. A prince! How could this little weed of a bird be a prince–a king-in-waiting? Wiping the tears from his eyes, Charlie puffed up his chest and reaching into the bag, pulled out *The Book of Dreams*. "Now me hearties, I'll check the story," he said, getting into character. "It's bound to tell us something." Charlie opened the book to the next point in the story but all it said was:

Close your eyes, Charlie Ramsbottom.

So Charlie closed his eyes. The others waited, Moon a tad impatiently. "Well," said the irritated eaglet, unable to stand it any longer. "What's happening?"

Charlie opened his eyes wide and spoke.

"All I saw was a picture of a fox, a fox flying. It's crazy, I know, but that's what I saw."

"It's an omen," said Noni Benoni in a reverent tone. "Show them, Eric."

"Come with me," said Mr. Grumblebum. They followed him to the rear of the house, and there at the end of the garden attached to a rusty steel pole and a departure platform was a cable swing device.

"In my younger days, that's how we used to get to school," said Noni. "It was very exciting and took me to within a few hundred yards of the school, just at the back of the forest.

Problem is, it was condemned as being unsafe. We never knew how long it would be until the cable might snap. It's all rusted now, very dangerous if you ask me," she said with a worried look on her face.

"It's their only chance," said Mr. Grumblebum. "If you take the flying fox, I'm sure you will see what's happening to the skateboard," he said. "Will you chance it, lad?" Charlie nodded his head but Moon was a little unsure.

"He's already tried to kill me three times. I'm a bird you know, not a cat. I've only got one life and that's already been stretched." Charlie translated.

"Oh, but I thought you were a king-in-waiting," said Noni, playing up to Moon's loftier nature. Moon made some squawking sounds. Charlie translated again.

"He said that he was only really worried about my safety, not his own."

"How admirable," the teacher and librarian said quietly, embracing the royal eagle and Charlie. Then they helped the two warriors climb the ladder to the flying machine. Noni Benoni kissed Charlie on the cheek and whispered in his ear, "Look after that bird; he's the next King."

"I don't know how to thank you," said Charlie, absorbing the goodness of Noni into his being. Again, the evil voice of Skunk Weavel began to torment him.

"Take the fox and on the way drop that pathetic bird into a rubbish dump."

"When we return from this quest," said Charlie. "My parents are going to give me the biggest birthday party this village has ever seen and you're both invited." Mr. Grumblebum shook

Charlie's hand and smiled encouragingly. He whispered into Charlie's ear the following words: "Pure heart—retain a pure heart and you will succeed." Moon thanked them with a flurry of his wings and the pair readied themselves for the journey on the flying fox. Charlie strapped the schoolbag across his body and Moon climbed onto his back. He grabbed the horizontal bar and Mr. Grumblebum pushed them away. In a trice, they were flying along the rusty cable which stretched out into nowhere through the blackness of the night.

Flying down the hill through the steamy night air, Charlie and Moon began to recognize landmarks: the school and the church and Smellie's Bakery, where they had hidden from the Snarlies.

They were just starting to enjoy the exhilaration of the flying fox when they spotted the skateboard speeding down the slope, gradually gathering speed as it headed towards checkpoint Snarlie. They could see the Snarlies sitting around a card table practicing a hand of Happy Families, totally unaware of what was bearing down on them.

Skunk's voice returned to eat at Charlie's sense of loyalty. This time it was unbelievably convincing. *"Throw the eagle down, down into the rubbish dump. Now! Now! Now! You will be king. Not that scrawny eagle. You will be all powerful."* For a moment, the lure of power almost swayed him at the thought of all he could have; he was about ready to dump the little pain. He turned to face Moon but the little fellow looked absolutely petrified and snuggled in close to him as they sped deeper and deeper into the night. It gave Charlie a feeling of comradeship and was enough to pull him back from the dark cave his mind was entering.

They sped companionably along when without warning, the flying fox abruptly emitted a large zinging sound and its cable split apart. Charlie and Moon were pinged, as if by a catapult, through the air and out of control, directly towards a hay cart that was parked on the side of the road.

Charlie hit the hay first, completely disappearing into the mass of thin yellow stalks. Moon followed close behind. He tried to fly but the speed of the ping was too much for him and he smashed into the spiky pile. The skateboard was getting faster by the minute and was not more than a hundred eagle hops from the Snarlies, who were so engrossed in their game that they didn't see, or even hear the commotion.

Slowly, Charlie raised his head out of the hay. Next to him lay a moaning Moon.

"When will you realize I am not a cat? I only have one life. One life! Do you understand?" Charlie felt for the bird.

"He almost got to you back there, didn't he?"

"Who?" said Charlie.

"You know who," said Moon. Charlie was about to respond when the voices of Flip and Flop grew louder, interrupting his thoughts. Raising his head over the edge of the hay cart, he could see Flop taking Flip through his version of Happy Families. Moon nestled into Charlie, watching Flop explaining his logic to Flip. Charlie realized that there was no other way past these two card-sharks but through the checkpoint. It was now or never. With Moon on his shoulder, he jumped out of the hay-cart into the middle of the road and walked boldly up to Skunk's heavies. Flip saw him first.

"Where you off to, pirate?" shouted the smelly vulture.

Charlie was sure he would be recognized. Out of the corner of his unpatched eye, he caught sight of the skateboard careening down the road towards them.

"Why me shipmates, me old, me old whachamacallits," he said nervously, avoiding the pungent odor of Flip's snout. "We're off to see the wizard, the wonderful wizard of..."

"O.K., that'll do. That'll do. What's the parrot's name?" said Flop. The board was getting closer by the second.

"Pieces of six, seven, I mean eight, you ignorant goon," screamed Moon. Flip immediately recognized Moon's voice and reached out to grab him when Charlie jumped back, seeing the board hurtling towards them like a rickety ball of greased lightning. Flip and Flop eyed Charlie for a split second before they too sensed that something was coming from behind them at hurt-speed. By the time they turned around, the skateboard was about half a worm's spit from their snouts, and realizing it could hit them, they dived tumbling and grumbling into a ditch by the side of the road. Charlie grabbed Moon and managed to jump onto the edge of the skateboard. In a flash, Charlie saw a slight ridge, aimed the skateboard towards it, and he and Moon went flying over the top of the floundering Snarlies.

"I'm losing control. We're going to crash!" shouted Charlie.

"No, we're not. Pull out the sail!" yelled Moon.

Charlie pulled on the lever and the sail immediately sprung into life, catching the wind and pushing the skateboard even faster towards the Plains of Desire. When Charlie and Moon hit the road they punched the air. Just then a loud clicking sound caught their attention. They were passing an airport-styled departure sign with letters that kept changing until it finally displayed the following message:

THE PLAINS OF DESIRE
Whatever you imagine
Can be yours...

Holding onto the skateboard sail for dear life, Charlie and Moon raced by the sign. Once past it, the board displayed the final part of its message. What Charlie and Moon did not see were the words:

...at a price!

Under the bright moonlight, the Plains looked very bare and seemed to reach out forever. Moon was very excited and exclaimed, "The skateboard's holding to the Plains. Just trust and let go."

Charlie released his grip on the sail and turned around to see if the Snarlies were following. "Skunk Weavel has no chance of getting us here," he said confidently just as a grubby hand with long fingernails reached out from thin air to tightly wrap itself around Moon's neck.

Chapter Ten: Brothers in Arms

The deathly white hand tightly gripped Moon's neck, trying to squeeze the life out of him. Instantly, Charlie karate chopped the grubby mitt as hard as he could. The hand screamed, hissed and then dissolved into dust. Moon lay on the skateboard shocked and shivering from the terrifying experience. He gulped in the cool night air and tried to breathe. Charlie picked up the little bird and held him, comforting him as best he could. The call had been close, but these were the Plains of Desire. No one traveled across the Plains because they were so dangerous. A few people had tried but had never returned. Rumor had it that the voices of the Plains had sent them crazy and literally ripped them apart, limb-by-limb.

As it entered the treacherous territory, the skateboard took on a life of its own. Moving like a speeding roller coaster, there was nothing that Charlie and Moon could do but to tightly hold onto each other. A sudden shift in the wind then brought them a most repulsive experience. A stench like mouldy, stinky, blue-vein cheese hit Charlie and Moon's nostrils. Immediately recognizing the smell, Moon cringed, saying that it was the odorous anger of Skunk Weavel. Having failed in his attempt to get rid of Moon, the toymaker had slunk back into his hole, leaving the putrid reek of hatred behind. "So *that's* why he's called *Skunk* Weavel," said Charlie taking out a large handkerchief from his pocket and wrapping it around his face like a bandit.

In the sky, large banks of clouds tussled with each other, flashing angry streaks of energy that electrified the night landscape. Charlie looked back to see if there was any sign of the Snarlies. There wasn't. What a relief. They could do without being chased by the two terrors for a while.

Rolling faster and faster across the Plains, in the distance they could see Old Sweeney's farm. Nine huge bonfires were burning in the fields. It was the season of goodwill and people were celebrating the solstice, completely unaware of the two adventurers and the perilous journey they were undertaking. Charlie felt Moon's head fall heavily into his shoulder and suddenly the bird was gone, sleeping to his heart's content. The minute Moon fell asleep; the Plains began whispering to Charlie.

**"...quincequonceeeee...eeeeat...the...
quincequoncee...quincequonceeeee...
eeeeat...the...quincequoncee..."**

Quickly, Charlie grabbed *The Book of Dreams* from his schoolbag. He knew he must not listen to the voices from The

Plains and had to put his attention elsewhere. He tried to open the book. At first the cover wouldn't budge. The whispering of the voices grew louder.

"...quincequonceeeee...eeeeat...the... quincequoncee...quincequonceeeee... eeeeat...the...quincequoncee..."

It was their sound. It got right into the marrow of your bones, ready to rip you apart at any moment. In a panic, Charlie finally pulled the pages open and for the moment, the voices of the plains faded away.

On the next page of *The Book* an unusual thing was happening. The story became alive as if again Charlie was watching a real-time movie. He saw a furious electrical storm illuminate the City of the Quincequonces, making it look like the keeper of nightmares had constructed it. Bolts of lightning momentarily turned the metropolis from night into day and back into night again before you could blink an eye. Within those split seconds of darkened iridescence, Charlie could just make out a dank cellar very carefully hidden under a brightly-lit toy factory with a flashy corporate looking sign that read 'ANIMALS-R-US.' The cellar was well away from public view and in that sad, dark cave, a magnificent eagle awoke to the sound of the storm's intermittent thunder. It was Listen-To-The-Wind, Moon's father and the great King of the Eagles. Listen-To-The-Wind looked around amidst the low harrumbling noise of his sleeping feathered comrades. To keep their snoring to a minimum, the eagles had painful pegs clipped tightly to their noses, a device conjured up for them by the evil Toyminator.

Charlie flipped over to the next page and saw that Listen-To-The-Wind was loosely chained to a stake. In the scene that played out before him, the sad old king arose and shuffled awkwardly across the cold cement floor to awaken his wife, I-Can-See-For-Miles. Before he could get to her, the chain tightened, stopping him from reaching his queen. Upon awakening, the queen rubbed her eyes and uttered her trademark refrain, "I have had a very interesting dream and I can see for miles." She picked up her spectacles and looked affectionately at her husband as he spoke his concerns to her.

"I'm worried about Moon. I shouldn't have sent him. I myself should have gone. If only..."

"Ssshhh," said his wife, now completely awake. "All is not lost. Remember the dream. I've a feeling that all will be well. This is as much Moon's story as it is Charlie Ramsbottom's." Just then, the trap door sprung open and Snarlie bird Flop hurtled through, crashing to the ground followed by an extremely irate Flip.

"You stupid fool, Flop," screamed Flip. "I had them in the palm of my claw and what did you do? You didn't tell me there was a skateboard rushing down the street about to run us over. I had the boy and the eagle, you whimpering piece of flaky toenail." Flop trembled at Flip's volcanic temper while Listen-To-The-Wind and I-Can-See-For-Miles looked at each other, excited by the news that Moon was on his way.

Flip let rip again. "You know what that means, Flop. It means that I'm probably going to have to socialize with those stupid Thunder Egg Chickens again to find out where that weedy little eagle is. But, and it's a big but: I'll beat them in the third game and show them who the real champion of Happy Families is." Flop turned away and smiled to himself, thinking of his chicky-baby, Runningmouth.

"Happy Families? Who's been playing Happy Families?" hissed a voice from behind them as it came down the cellar stairs. Charlie couldn't see the figure that had spoken but knew it had to be Skunk Weavel. Not only did the voice sound the same as the one that had whispered in his head, but a horrible cheesy smell began to emanate from the book's pages. A sense of revulsion pervaded Charlie's being. That the toymaker had nearly turned him against Moon was unthinkable, inexcusable. Charlie could have been lost to Skunk Weavel forever, never to see his parents again. The tears welled in his eyes but he quickly snapped out of his melancholy when Snarlie Flip replied to Skunk Weavel's question about the card game.

"Only a little teensy-weensy game your royal Toyminator, with two Thunder Egg Chickens, just to find out where…that irritating eagle might be hiding," whined the quivering Flip. And then in the darkened shadows of this impenetrable prison, a shaft of light flashed across Skunk's distorted face, briefly revealing a tongue that danced around like a tormented worm, sliming its way up to the bridge of the toymaker's nose and back again. It was as if Skunk's face was shaking off some incurable disease.

Flip and Flop turned on each other. "It was his fault," they cried out together, waving their claws in the other's direction. Skunk Weavel towered over the two Snarlies.

"Remember, Bird-Brains, I saved you two from the rubbish heap so don't let me down now. Find that stupid half-wit of an eagle, and as you seem to like Thunder Egg Chickens so much, bring me back a couple. I reckon they'd sell really well." Skunk turned so he was just in profile. Once again, his tongue danced in and out of his huge mouth. Suddenly opening wider, like a garbage disposal truck, it released a laugh that sounded not dissimilar to a demented hyena. With his madness increasing by the minute, Skunk pushed the two Snarlies out of the trap door.

All this time, Listen-To-The-Wind and I-Can-See-For-Miles had been watching the toymaker and the Snarlies. Skunk Weavel turned and saw that the two eagles were awake. He got down on bended knees and looked right into their eyes. Now Charlie was host to the full force of Skunk Weavel's ugly protuberance of a face. With teeth chock-a-block full of rotting food that would have been misery even for the toughest toothbrush to remove, the toymaker thundered out a warning. "The potion will soon be ready. Then I'm going to ram it down all of your lovely little throats and slowly turn you into...cuddly stuffed eagles." Listen-To-The-Wind tried to head-butt Skunk but the chains restricted him. I-Can-See-For-Miles took up the fight.

"Don't you worry, Skunk. Our boy will return with help and all the animals will rise up and turn *you* into a stuffed toymaker. And...it's not over until this fat eagle sings!" Skunk Weavel thought this highly amusing and began to laugh and hiss. He looked at the Queen and growled, "Get ready to sing, then, Fatso. Get ready!"

All of a sudden, there was a jolt and the skateboard slowed to a halt opposite a small clearing. Charlie looked up from the book, his face completely distraught. He felt as if his own heart had almost been corrupted by the toymaker. Ashamed, he felt a heavy sadness. At the same time, Moon awoke from his slumber. In front of them lay the remains of a fire. In the flickering light they could see paper plates and half eaten pieces of cake, now crawling with ants and cockroaches, strewn across the ground. Full bottles of sparkling apple juice sat open next to empty glasses. Slashed through the middle of this circle of picnic hampers and upturned wicker chairs was a trail of green gooba. Charlie picked up a few tufts of hair — teddy bear hair. This was where the last tribe of teddy bears had been Snarlied while they were having a late afternoon picnic. Charlie and Moon didn't say a word to each other, they were too shell-shocked by the kidnap of the defenseless bears, defenseless because eagles were no longer around to patrol the skies and warn them of any impending attacks.

The skateboard seemed to call the pair to move on and they did so, in absolute silence, eyes glazed as they passed through the pitch-black landscape. Numbed, Charlie re-opened the book. The story had moved from the cellar to Skunk Weavel's huge storeroom, the place where the animals were herded when they first entered the premises. There they were given the evil potion and placed on a conveyor belt by robots that very neatly positioned them on shelves so that customers could have the optimum retail therapy experience. In this prison camp atmosphere, the toymaker worked and sang to himself over a large cauldron of bubbling liquid. Charlie could just make out the words of the song:

Old Mac...Old Skunk Weavel, had a farm,

ee-eye, ee-eye oh

And on that farm he had an eagle, ee-eye, ee-eye oh

With a squawk, squawk here and a screech, screech there

Here a squawk, there a screech

Everywhere a squawk, screech

Old Skunk Weavel had a farm, ee-eye, ee-eye oh

While he worked, Skunk would often pause to tweak his flaky moustache with those awful fingers and to smile that unbelievable looking coat-hanger smile of his. Then with one of his long fingernails, he would pull a giant cruncher of dried wax from out of his ear, take a quick look to either side to make sure no one was watching and then pop the imitation ginger-looking mass onto his tongue and suck lustily on it as if it were boiled candy.

Behind the toymaker, in huge open storage cupboards that seemed to go on forever were rows upon rows of confounded koala bears, frightened flamingos, cheerless chipmunks, terrorized tree kangaroos, paralyzed penguins, squirming squirrels, wide-eyed wombats, edgy elephants, chastised cheetahs, tired Tasmanian tigers, intimidated iguanas, sorrowful snow leopards, beaten bandicoots, petrified pandas, joyless jaguars, pitiful polar bears, guarded gorillas and the last tribe of tortured teddy bears. The bears had put up a good fight but were no match for the evil ways of the toymaker. All of the cuddly stuffed animals peered at Weavel from inside their rigidified bodies and thought about revenge. Skunk didn't know this, and even if he had he wouldn't care. He laughed, cackled loudly to himself and began a ritual that Charlie could hardly comprehend as he watched it unfold, gagging, yet unable to look away.

First, from one of his enormous feet, Skunk Weavel slid off a mouldy-smelling, cheesified sock. Disgusting! The toymaker's toes were like little white maggots as they squirmed about in the harsh fluorescent light. Very carefully, Skunk dunked the limp and ragged sock ceremoniously into a mug of hot water, held it there for thirty seconds or so, squeezed it out and slid it back onto his foot.

Next, he added some out-of-date, tinned-milk to the mixture and two tablespoons of lice-infested brown sugar. Licking his moustache, just below the line of his red bulbous nose where the black hairs protruded like a colony of flies' legs, he stirred this nightly refreshment, energetically clunking the spoon noisily against the china receptacle.

Then, closing his reptilian-like eyes, Skunk Weavel put the mug to his frosted lips and sipped the cheesy tea. When the thick brown concoction passed into his cavernous gob, his eyes lit up like the brake lights of a car on a dark night. A beautiful brew if ever there was one. But he wasn't finished yet.

Reaching into a cupboard, Skunk pulled out a small soiled package encased in old newspaper. Slowly, he undid the crinkled wrapping. Rotting within the newsprint were some moth-eaten sandwiches, actually crawling with wriggly things! Black maggots!!! Dribbling oodles of saliva from the corner of his lips, the toymaker ripped off a piece of one of the mouldy sandwiches and popped it into his atrocious mouth and let out another devastating cackle. Wasn't life wonderful!

Peering up from the antique book, Charlie's face was as white as a ghost. He looked positively sick.

"That's the most disgusting thing I have ever seen," he said, completely overwhelmed by the experience.

"Then you've seen the enemy," replied Moon.

"Well, I've seen bits of him...the flies' legs from his nose...and those horrible feet," moaned Charlie.

Just then, from within the book, the bell sounded from the front of the shop. Someone had entered and was waiting to be served. Skunk composed himself. Calming his face, which in truth, resembled a bagful of wrenches, the toymaker's slippery eel-like tongue slid back into his mouth and he became your "most 'umble servant, sir" as he prepared to make another sale of his popular life-like toys.

C C C C

Back at the Ramsbottom residence, Penelope made her way quietly down the stairs, being careful not to disturb her parents who were watching yet another episode of *Talk with the Animals*. Dressed in black from head to toe, her face was covered with ghostly white facepaint. She carried Charlie's Lucky skateboard and opening the front door very slowly, she headed out to the chicken coop and made her way stealthily down the hill. Snoozeball and Runningmouth, who were on night-watch, heard Penelope enter the coop. Through a crack in the chicken dormitory door, they watched her push against the wall, frantically talking to herself the whole time. "I'm gonna get that Creep brother of mine. It's my turn now. Just you wait and see." The wall slid open revealing the passageway. "Take me to where the Creepoid is." She strode through and disappeared. Snoozeball and Runningmouth looked anxiously at each other, eyebrows raised in fear. Quietly they opened the dormitory door and followed Penelope down the passageway.

☾ ☾ ☾ ☾

The skateboard, which was now on a hill, slowed again for a few seconds. On the distant horizon, Charlie and Moon saw an unearthly red glow—a glow that radiated from the huge sky-scraping buildings of the City of the Quincequonces as they pierced a dirty grey mist that shrouded the stainless-steel metropolis. Charlie and Moon became still. They were about to enter a world of cheats and robbers, liars and thieves, dentists and doctors, accountants and lawyers, bankers, blackguards and politicians. They could turn back and people would say that they had done well to have made it this far. Charlie's heart raced. After what he had witnessed from within the pages of *The Book*, he was now ready to take on the evil Skunk Weavel, free all the animals and reunite *The Book of Dreams*.

With these thoughts passing through Charlie's mind, the skateboard rolled on. Moon looked at Charlie and smiled. His friend had reached a most important turning point. Soon though, the real battle would commence, a battle that would pit friend against friend and brother against sister. The Plains of Desire began to whisper and reach out to Charlie again. Moon urged him to turn to the next page in the book.

The bizarre tale now took Charlie Ramsbottom inside Skunk's shop. An elderly man had entered the premises. He had a white snowstorm of a beard and wore a heavy greatcoat. The man stood opposite the counter, whispering poetically to the stuffed animals, all crammed like sardines onto display shelves that seemed to reach for the sky.

"Don't worry my furry and feathered friends, for this is the day young Charlie Ramsbottom's coming your way," softly spoke the man. Although they couldn't move, the toys' eyes lit up when they saw this gentle man and heard his news. He continued quietly. "He'll be here real soon, so just keep calm. You'll be out of this fix, and he'll take you to his farm."

Sir Edward Bainbridge, the monocled leader of the teddy bears, looked into the gentleman's sad and watery eyes and whispered an urgent plea back to him. (To anyone else it would have sounded as though he was gagged and bound, but the old man got every word.)"Weally, old chap. Just get us out of this tewibble pwedicament so we can..." At that moment, Skunk Weavel walked through the door wearing a grimey white lab coat and whistling his theme song of *Old Macdonald Had a Farm*.

"Can I help you, Sir?" droned the toymaker, smiling a crooked set of teeth at the visitor. The man in the greatcoat turned and stared at Skunk. Skunk scowled at him.

"What do you want Nicholas *Bizz-Buzz*, Mr. Goodie-Two Shoes? I suppose you've come to scrounge money for another one of your hopeless charitable causes, eh?" Skunk threw an old bronze coin in Bizz-Buzz's direction, but Bizz-Buzz let it hit the floor. He took off his bright white gloves, and bowed to Skunk Weavel.

Charlie pulled back as the book shook violently in his hands. *This* was the mysterious Bizz-Buzz. Right in front of his very eyes. Charlie looked at Bizz-Buzz and then at Skunk and then back to Bizz-Buzz again. And if you had looked as closely as Charlie had, you would have detected a startling resemblance between the two men, mainly in the coloring of the eyes. They could have been brothers, so alike in appearance were they! Yet, how could they be? One so evil, the other so good! But it was true! The two men were actually born of the same mother! Peas from the very same pod!

The elder of the brothers, Bizz-Buzz, stood there for a moment looking at his younger brother, the wily and evil Skunk Weavel. Bizz-Buzz was always nervous in his brother's presence. He remembered their youth, when he constantly tried to stop his younger brother from trying to denude flies or cook live frogs or salamanders. Bizz-Buzz shuddered, recalling the day his brother stole into his beloved apiary to try to pull the wings off the Queen Bee just to get to Bizz-Buzz. The angry colony of bees attacked and stung the nasty boy all over his body, particularly his face. Skunk exploded in pain and rage, threatening revenge on every creature of earth, sky and sea. Little Doreen, who had been hiding in the corner of the apiary sucking on a honeycomb, witnessed the whole dreadful event and was so afraid of her Uncle Skunk that her knees trembled from that day onward. The bees swarmed around her, protecting her, nestling in her tower of thick hair. And it seemed that since that day, Skunk put a sting into everything he did.

Looking around in despair at the trapped animals in Skunk's factory, Bizz-Buzz also painfully recalled the days of their apprenticeship at the Gracelands Magic Toy Emporium. Having completely lost his marbles, Skunk (self-named after the only animal he could abide, due to its horrific rear-end odor, which he often tried to imitate) had stolen and drugged people's pets and secretly sold them to the selfish children of the rich and hideous. Sadly, his parents had no other choice but to tell him to leave. He swore he would avenge his humiliation and show them that his way was the best way, the only way to make toys, real stuffed toys.

So nervous was Bizz-Buzz right there in front of Skunk that he had to suck in a huge breath before he began speaking. "Brother, I have come to offer you a chance. Return the half of the book that you have and all will be well."

"What book, Nicholas?" asked the toymaker innocently.

Bizz-Buzz stood on one side of the counter absolutely still. Skunk stood on the other. They looked squarely into each other's eyes. In this wicked den of darkness, Bizz-Buzz summoned up his courage once more. "Beware, because you know not the forces that you meddle with. The boy has a noble power growing within him."

Like the true salesman he was, Skunk played Bizz-Buzz like the Devil's fiddler. He had infiltrated young Ramsbottom's mind and the book would soon be his. Still, he didn't want to spoil Bizz-Buzz's little melodrama, so he continued the ruse. Bizz-Buzz bizzed his brother again. "He'll follow his heart to higher ground and see you for what you are. And then you won't stand a chance."

Skunk made his face turn a little red, pretending to be angry with his brother.

"Book! What book? What boy? What are you talking about, you old fool?" he said, hardly able to restrain himself from laughing.

Bizz-Buzz continued very deliberately knowing that what he was about to say would push his brother over the edge. "It's time to stop being a schemer. You haven't a chance. You're up against…the magic of a…dreamer!"

Shocked out of his indifference, Skunk's hands raced to cover his ears. His blood pressure increased dramatically so that his face became an even deeper shade of red. If there was one thing he hated, really, really hated, it was dreamers. Dreamers were useless (like Bizz-Buzz), prone to having much too much imagination. Life was meant to be serious, not light-hearted. The bottom line was how much money you made, how powerful you were, and Skunk hated dreamers as much as the next factory sweat shop owner. His motto was "Stop dreaming and stay on the job." Just the idea of dreaming started making him shake as if he were having a conniption fit. He began shouting at Bizz-Buzz and let rip with tornado-like anger.

"Get out of here, you old codger! Go on, get lost!" he screamed and hissed. "And buy yourself a new coat! You look ridiculous!"

Saddened by his brother's refusal to listen to reason (even a little), Bizz-Buzz bowed dramatically and left the premises. When Bizz-Buzz closed the door behind him, a great arc of lightning bolted down from the sky, temporarily zizzing up the shop like someone taking a photograph with a huge flashbulb.

The flash was too strong for Charlie. The book jumped out of his hands and fell onto the skateboard. What Charlie didn't see in the flash of light was a pair of eyes peering out of the shadows from the doorway of the next shop.

Quickly, Charlie picked up the book and re-opened it. By this time, Skunk Weavel was sitting, calming himself down and sipping his cheesy tea. He composed himself, sucked in an enormous breath of putrid air that made the curtains flutter, and then stared deep into the recesses of his mind. There didn't seem to be anything that could prevent him from achieving control over *The Book of Dr...* He couldn't even allow himself to think of the word Drea...The other half of the book was being personally delivered to him by the Ramsbottom kid and that's all that mattered. It was slowly becoming *The Book of Skunk Weavel Rules*. Surely, nothing could go wrong. Or could it? Maybe it could. But what was he to do?

For a while it seemed that the lights had gone out in the toymaker's brain. Then slowly but ever so surely, his eyes began to flicker. An ugly smile filled his mouth. You could see the germ of an idea forming in his sinister mind. His tongue started dancing about again. Excitedly, he picked up an unusual striped piece of fruit and rammed it into his mouth, making the purple juice pour down from his refrigerated lips onto to his greasy lab coat. Skunk's body raised itself up high above the counter and let out a Ferocious Attack of The Roaring Trumpets, which almost blew Charlie off the board. At the same time, Skunk's face took on a disgusting smirk.

"Nothing like a quincequonce to get one's thoughts moving," chortled Skunk. "I feel like a new toymaker again." With an air of nonchalance, Skunk reached across to a two-way radio and called up the Snarlies.

"Skunk Weavel to Bird-Brain One. Skunk Weavel to Bird-Brain One. Over."

"One Bird-Brain. I hear you loud and clear, Master. Over," came the static-filled response.

"Listen carefully, Flip, you imbecilic bird-brain. I've decided to move the plans forward and..." Without warning, the sound from the book diminished to an inaudible whisper. Charlie could see the mouth of the toymaker moving but could not make out the words that were dribbling from his lips. Then, just as quickly as the sound had faded, so it returned. Skunk let out a bloodcurdling laugh and returned to the back of the factory to finish mixing his evil potion. Charlie stared long into the book, but as the pages faded into blackness and Skunk disappeared from view, he suddenly heard the Plains of Desire whispering to him again:

"...quincequonceeeee... eeeeat... the... quincequoncee...quincequonceeeee... eeeeat...the...quincequoncee..."

Then Charlie felt something creepy, really creepy, crawling slowly up his leg.

Chapter Eleven: Facing the Quincequonces

When Charlie looked down he saw, much to his surprise, a small purple and red-striped, octopus-like fruit slowly climbing up his body. Around him, the Plains of Desire were covered with the most horrid grey-colored bushes and trees bearing fruit whose aroma was surprisingly delicious, like banana and chocolate custard with jellybeans and sherbet fizzers. Charlie couldn't resist eating the piece that was walking across his tummy and quickly popped it into his mouth. With his taste buds surrounded by the succulent fruit, attacking and squeezing out its edible life force, Charlie Ramsbottom went into a heavenly spin. This was the most awesome gastronomic sensation he had ever experienced. It made him feel like a king—as if he could do anything. And then another one was sliding up his arm, almost smiling at him. He was just about to pick up this delectable piece of juiciness and slam it into his mouth when a claw ripped it away. "It's a quincequonce, you fool," squawked Moon. "The forbidden fruit! The Plains are playing with you!"

"Don't be ridiculous," replied Charlie, all in a swoon. "It's splendilectable. The perfect meal all rolled into one."

"I hope you haven't eaten any," said a worried Moon.

"Yes, I have and I'm going to have another and another," said Charlie, reaching for a bunch of quincequonces that hung from a branch just above his head. Moon, greatly dismayed, squawked noisily, stopping Charlie in the nick of time.

"If you've only eaten one, we've a chance," the bird cried.

"What do you mean?" queried an annoyed Charlie as he started to feel the first signs of painful spots and bumps erupting on his face.

"Eat too many quincequonces and you'll become a Quincequoncian, which means you'll grow ugly and cheat and lie. And you'll start having Ferocious Attacks of the Roaring Trumpets, which means that the air around you will always be toxic and dirty. And bit by bit your body will reject and disown you." Charlie could already feel his body loosening at the joints.

"Oh dear," cried Moon." It's already happening. Look at your face! Oh, your arms, your legs too! And your stomach— it's getting ready to explode!"

Feeling more volcanic bumps starting to protrude from the skin on his face, Charlie suddenly understood the meaning of a Ferocious Attack of the Roaring Trumpets. A sound like a thousand snorting wild pigs, riding on gas-guzzling motorbikes suddenly shot out from underneath his trousers leaving him weak and all asunder. That's why an attack of the roaring trumpets was ferocious—too many of them and you were sure to collapse from exhaustion and their awful stench.

But the fruit: it tasted so wonderful.

While Charlie pondered his immediate fate, the skateboard reached the very edge of the City of the Quincequonces. The air was dense with a slimy residue and the quincequonce bushes and trees had become larger and larger, smelling more delicious than ever, forming a canopy over the Plains of Desire. Charlie, desirous of another taste and so distracted by the quincequonce's beautiful aroma, had to ram two fingers up his nose to ward off the enticing smell.

Within a hundred eagle hops, the skateboard began to steer them out of the Plains, but not before a thousand skeletal hands reached out to pull them back. The two adventurers fought and fought to break away from the screeching hands, karate chopping, biting and clawing at each creepy hand until they broke loose. Finally, they were free and skated through the outskirts of the metropolis, beyond the dirt-stained, marbled walls that protected the city from outsiders. Charlie, however, was no longer an outsider. He had become an honorary Quincequoncian by merit of partaking of the forbidden fruit, and he continued to be reminded of that honor every few steps by involuntarily letting rip with Ferocious Attacks of the Roaring Trumpets.

In the city (that seemed to be held together by chewing gum and elastic bands) there was a general buzz of excitement and a party spirit in the air. Christmas was coming, which was an excuse for the local residents to stuff their faces with the most delectable variations of quincequonce dishes. Looking around the tall buildings, Charlie and Moon could see a group of obesely bulbous, nose dribbling Quincequoncians making their way home from their late-night partying at local

quincequonce bars. All were full with the latest culinary fare—
crème de le quincequonce - and all were having ferocious attacks
of numerous roaring trumpets, which they found uproariously
funny. Some of them were even being pushed home in
shopping-carts, they were that full and exhausted. Of course,
no one paid much attention to the boy pirate and the parrot
with two Thunder Eggs on an oversized skateboard.

When the last group of the Quincequoncians finally
disappeared into the darkened alleys that led to their homes,
the streets suddenly became terribly empty and deserted. Wind
tunnels, created by the tall buildings, sucked in the night vapors
from off the plains. The air whistled through the streets,
simultaneously adding to the stench from the rotten roaring
trumpet odor.

Charlie kicked off and the skateboard started to move again,
guiding him and Moon past the massive wooden gates of a
large toy-world theme park partially hidden by boards and
workmen's scaffolding. Festooned on one of the walls outside
the gates were large posters that read:

Weavel World
Grand Opening – Tomorrow

Skunk Weavel's disgusting face was central in all of the
posters, with an unhappy looking entourage of Moon's family
and friends surrounding the Toyminator. This upset Moon
terribly and he started to whimper.

"Don't cry Moon. We'll save them. I can feel it in my blood," said a nauseated Charlie, guiding the board underneath the cover of a bridge. The bridge spanned what used to be a vibrant river, but which was now only a streak of yellow grime that snaked its desperate way through the city. Along the banks of the river lay dead, rotting fish, washed up against the withered trunks of formerly proud weeping willows. All the willows could do now was to weep tears of distress. Deeply affected by the carnage around him, Charlie opened the book once more. An important message appeared at the bottom of the page:

You have done well so far.
There are only three hours to go.
Whoever owns the book protects the dreaming.
It's time for action!

Still sick to his stomach, Charlie saw the chocolates that Noni Benoni had packed in his bag, and the flask with the tea concoction that Mr. Grumblebum had made. The flask read: Antidote for F.A.R.T.s. Charlie gratefully drank the antidote tea, which helped to allay the effects of the quincequoncian fruit. He inwardly thanked his insightful teachers. While Charlie re-read the message and drank his tea, Moon munched on the chocolates. Suddenly, there was a wheezing and a whining from overhead. Flip and Flop had landed on the bridge above them. Charlie and Moon slid into the shadows and listened to their regurgitative conversation.

"One Bird-Brain to the Master. One Bird-Brain to the Master." Flip was on his two-way radio to the diabolical

Toyminator. "We're on the bridge. No sign of the enemy. Repeat. No sign of the enemy. One Bird-Brain out and over from the bridge." Charlie and Moon didn't know it, but Flip gave Flop one of those winks of the eye that said, 'We know where they are but we're just pretending that we don't.' The two birds flew off blabbering, prattling and arguing. Charlie thought he heard Flop saying to his partner, "Why did you wink at me?"

Checking to see that they were safe to move from their position, Charlie and Moon slowly crept out from their hiding place. Charlie gave the skateboard a push, but it seemed strangely reluctant to move.

"O.K. Moon. Time's running short. How do we get to Skunk Weavel's factory?" whispered Charlie.

"I don't know. I thought you knew," Moon replied, shivering in the wind.

"That's great," said Charlie. "Less than three hours to go and we're lost."

Moon was almost apologetic. "Look Charlie, it's not my fault...I thought..."

"O.K., O.K. Moon," replied Charlie, a little irritated. "The book says I have to take action. So there's only one thing to do now."

"What's that?" asked Moon. Charlie's bottom lip turned up. He had a look of steely determination in his eye and nodded his head in quiet self-congratulation as he spoke.

"Ask for directions," he said, finding it increasingly difficult to push the board out into the open square. By now it was just past nine o'clock, and the city was filled with a frightening quiet. The street lamps flickered. Wisps of smoke poured from out of storm water drains in an alley opposite to where Charlie and Moon stood.

"Ask directions from whom...where?" queried Moon. Desperately, Charlie looked around. Right opposite them was an old bookshop. The lamps were still burning.

"Look. Over there," said Charlie pointing to the shop. "Maybe it's still open. I'm sure someone in the bookshop will know how to get to Skunk Weavel's." He tried to hurry the stubborn skateboard over to the shop but it wouldn't move. He tried again. Still it wouldn't budge.

"Wait here while I go inside and ask for directions," he said to Moon.

"It doesn't feel good to me," replied the eagle.

"Oh, don't be so silly," said Charlie. "I'm only going to go and ask the way. What could happen?" Charlie was impatient and did not heed Moon's warning. Still holding the book, he ran across the square, making a beeline for the crusty looking shop. Within two eagle hops, he was there.

Very cautiously, he opened the door and entered the premises. A strange, bell-like twang sounded just above his head as he walked across squeaky floorboards to the counter. Around him were towering piles of old dusty books, and antique-type tomes, all covered with cobwebs and all leaning inwards, looking like they were about to fall over. It reminded him of Noni Benoni's living room. Charlie felt an urge to run back out again, but when he turned, there was Moon waving at him from across the square. He waved back, smiling. He didn't realize Moon's frantic claw signal was telling him to get out, fast!

Charlie noticed a woman standing behind the counter. She had her back to him and from where she stood, Charlie thought she looked very much like Noni Benoni. What a wonderful coincidence! Humming to herself, she was looking in a box full of books. Charlie cleared his throat to get "Noni's" attention, but she continued to sift through the books, ignoring him. Charlie coughed a little louder. Still the woman ignored him. Charlie put his half of *The Book of Dreams* down on top of some other books next to the counter, cupped his hands into a bullhorn and shouted out, "Noni, is that you? It's me, Charlie." The woman answered Charlie without turning around.

"No need to shout. I can hear you," she said, her voice vaguely familiar. As she spoke, the woman depressed a concealed lever on the floor. Utterly undetected by Charlie, his half of *The Book of Dreams* dropped from the counter only to be replaced by a fake.

"What can I do for you?"enquired the woman, rather cheerfully, but still not turning around.

"Can you tell me how to get to Skunk Weavel's toyshop?"

"There's a bus stop around the corner," she replied, gesturing with her hand. "Wait there and take the first bus."

"Thank you. Thank you very much," said Charlie taking his leave.

"Stop!" shouted the woman. Charlie stopped in his tracks. "Don't forget your book."

"Oh, thank you *ever* so much," said Charlie, relieved he hadn't forgotten *The Book of Dreams*.

Charlie left the shop, gripping the book tightly with both hands. Once he had closed the door behind him, the woman took her head out of the box of books and began humming her tune a little louder. The tune was *Old Macdonald...* and upon close inspection you could see that the woman had a large cluster of flies' legs sprouting out from her huge nostrils. "Noni" turned around and ripped off her mask. There, revealed, was none other than Skunk Weavel dressed to look like Noni Benoni. Skunk held up one half of *The Book* in his right hand and the other half in his left and let out a cackle of laughter that brought tears of joy to his eyes.

Back outside in the cold dank air, Charlie ran back to Moon.

"Well?" asked Moon. "What happened?"

"I got directions," said Charlie. "It was easy."

He pushed the now agreeable skateboard towards the bus stop. "It's just over here...around this corner," said a self-satisfied Charlie to Moon when they neared the platform. But when they looked at the timetable that was hanging from an old wooden post, it showed them a picture of a snake with the letters S.W. engraved upon it.

"What happened in that shop?" squawked an extremely concerned Moon. Charlie looked back around the corner towards the shop and saw that the lights had gone out. Very quietly, and finding it hard to run his sentences together, Charlie told Moon what had occurred.

"You fool! Don't you think if it was Noni Benoni, she would have said something to you!" shouted Moon. "The book, check the book!" Charlie opened the bogus *Book of Dreams*. Inside was a picture of Skunk Weavel, dancing maniacally and laughing at them. The rotter had stolen Charlie's half! He had been tricked and had to get the book back! He was its keeper! Tearfully, he remembered the last message from its pages, repeating it softly to himself,

Whoever owns the book protects the dreaming.

Now the book was in Skunk's possession and he could do what he liked. He would never protect the dreaming. He would control it!

"Oh Moon! I've made a terrible, terrible mistake," cried Charlie. "I let Skunk Weavel trick me and now he's got the book! We've got to get to the shop before he does!" As if on cue, the No. 9 bus came hurtling around the corner.

"Come on, we'll take this bus." Moon stood there like a stone statue. He had gone into shock and was utterly speechless!

Placing Moon gently on the board next to the Thunder Eggs, Charlie prepared to jump on the bus. But the bus didn't stop; it slowly passed them by. With no time to lose, Charlie chased after the vehicle, pushing the skateboard along with all his might. Somehow, he clambered on board and hitched the long board to the back of the bus as only an eagle scout could. As the bus picked up speed, Charlie lifted a stunned Moon into his arms and took his seat. Charlie hoped the eggs were still secure enough to withstand yet another jostling ride.

Looking around at the inside of the bus, Charlie felt that he had seen this bus somewhere before. The strange-looking ticket collector was wearing an eye mask and a red polka dotted headscarf over her enormous head of hair that housed a swarm of honeybees. Dancing on the spot in front of them, she chewed on a piece of honeycomb as she enquired as to their destination. Charlie hesitated before he spoke. Could this masked lone ranger be trusted? His mind was all over the place and he was in no fit state to make rational judgments. He had just given *The Book of Dreams* to Skunk Weavel. It didn't matter that it was done accidentally. Someone had to be trusted and he wasn't the one—that was for certain. Unable to contain his thoughts any longer, his mouth sprang open and the words jumped out like a boxing kangaroo.

"Skunk Weavel's factory please," said Charlie, looking at the woman with suspicion.

"Don't you mean ANIMALS-R-US?" she asked.

"Yup, that's the place."

She shivered, nodding, "Oooh, that slimy toymaker, what he's going to do in that Weavel World...and his stuffed toys...they look so...so...so...."

"Real. Yeah I know," said Charlie, sadly finishing off the sentence. The ticket collector, who was in the middle of a salsa, slowed her dancing down. Charlie noticed that the bus slowed down too.

"I've always thought that he...," she said, her knees trembling. And then she stopped, summoned by a fear from within that she shouldn't speak out loud. She changed the subject. "Well, let's see. A pirate, a parrot and a skateboard to go one hundred eagle hops. That'll be two banana milkshakes, please." She broke into a square dance, do-si-do-ing up and down the aisle. The bus started to speed up once again.

"Two banana milkshakes?" asked Charlie, incredulously. "I don't have that kind of money on me. I could do an impersonation of them, I suppose." So Charlie stood up and tried to do an impersonation of two banana milkshakes.

"No. Not good enough," said the conductress, switching to a livelier dance step. "How much money do you have?" Now the bus was tearing along.

"Actually, I don't have any money at all," said Charlie.

"Well, how are you going to pay?" she asked, moving effortlessly into a waltz. The bus slowed down. Charlie thought for a moment and worriedly scratched his head. Then a most wonderful solution floated into his brain. Every morning before breakfast, his parents would put on their favorite country and western medley and dance their hearts out in the living room on a special handmade carpet imported from Mr. Ramsbottom's native Scotland. Sometimes, Charlie would join them. With these thoughts flashing through his mind and sensing an ally in the woman, Charlie stood up.

"There's only one way I know how to pay," he said bravely. "Would you like this dance?" The ticket collector was taken aback. "My parents are the Country and Western Ballroom Dance champions of Thunder Egg Downs," Charlie stated confidently. "I assure you, I'm very good."

Under her mask, the woman blushed. "In all my years on this bus, nine years in fact, this is the first time anyone has offered to partner me. It must be an omen," she said adjusting her beehive hair. Through her mask, tears welled in her eyes, and taking Charlie's hand, they began a Country and Western barn dance down the aisle of the bus.

Moon sat in his seat, completely amazed. *The Book of Dreams* had been stolen. His family was about to be turned into stuffed toys and all Charlie could do was dance with a strange-looking ticket collector. Wide-eyed and steaming, he watched them talking as they glided up and down the narrow passageway but couldn't hear a word until the end of the medley when the woman curtsied to Charlie.

"That's a deal," she said, starting up another dance while Charlie bowed. "Now, you'd better jump off here. Quick! I don't want any trouble." She looked nervously around and then rang the bell. The bus slowed, but didn't actually stop. Only then did Charlie notice that the bus didn't have a driver.

"Where's the bus driver?" Charlie enquired.

"She's here," said the ticket collector, ripping off her mask and scarf. It was none other than Doreen Tremblingknees. Before Charlie could ask for an explanation, Doreen yelled out excitedly, "You'd better get ready to jump off. We're almost there. We're almost there!"

Holding Moon with one hand, Charlie unhitched the skateboard, and grabbing it tightly, pulled it alongside the edge of the buses' platform.

"Go, Charlie Ramsbottom. Go, you little sweet thang!" called out Doreen.

"Careful now, careful," said Charlie to himself as he lowered Moon onto the board. Then he jumped onto their faithful transporter and let go. As the bus pulled away, he turned and shouted after Doreen, "Don't forget, will you!" She called back after them, "I won't forget, eagle boy! Don't worry, I will remember you with all my heart... and watch the hill, it's very steep."

Then the bus disappeared from view.

"Eagle boy? Hill. What hill?" Charlie shouted after the bus, but when he and Moon turned around to see where they were headed, their sweet little good-bye smiles were suddenly windblown into a blur of lip-and-beak-flapping babble with a G-force that almost tore the breath right out of their lungs. They were speeding full pelt, downhill. The road flashed by under the wheels of the long board. A large red neon sign, which was drawing closer by the second, flashed out the words,

ANIMALS-R-US...ANIMALS-R-US.

The skateboard was accelerating faster and faster. They were only ten eagle hops from the huge store window when, for the very first time, Charlie could see that devil of a toymaker in all his glory.

Dressed in his stained lab technician's coat with his slick flock of black hair and its distinct white stripe, Skunk Weavel was sitting on a large throne-styled chair reading from *The Book of Dreams* to a young girl attired in black. The scoundrel!

Five eagle hops from the window, Charlie racked his brains for a way out of the situation. But the girl, the young girl! There was something about her. She had her back to the window and was talking and laughing outrageously with the toymaker.

The girl! The girl! Who was she? He'd seen her before. He was sure of it! But where? When? Two and a half eagle hops to go. Faster and faster. Just at that very moment, with the skateboard ready to crash right through the exact center of the plate glass window, the girl turned around to face them. She was cuddling a brand new stuffed teddy bear. How awful! When she saw Charlie, and before Skunk Weavel was even aware of what was happening, she let out the loudest silent scream you ever heard. Through the window, Charlie could virtually see what she had for breakfast.

His eyes super-sized: his jaw bungee-dropped. He couldn't believe it. The girl was none other than his sister, Penelope!

Chapter Twelve: The Call of the Conch

At one solitary eagle hop from Skunk Weavel's plate glass window, Charlie's only thought should have been the fact that he and Moon were about to crash right through the store front window, but all he could really think about and really see was his sister, laughing and joking with the Toyminator. Moon fluttered his wings furiously, trying to fly free but the parrot outfit weighed him down and kept him board bound.

"Charlie! Get us out of this mess," he screamed. "Do something. This instant! Do something!" But Charlie's jaw was dropping further and further from his top lip, almost to his knees. Then Moon remembered the Conch of the Great Ocean. Furiously clawing at Charlie's bag, within milli-pilli seconds he found the shell, plucked it free and rammed it into Charlie's mouth—all in one motion.

"Charlie Ramsbottom," yelled Moon. "This is an order. Blow as hard as you can. NOW!" Moon shouted so loudly, he even surprised himself. They were only an ant's breath away from total disaster.

When the taste of the conch crossed his lips, a distinct smell of sea and salt surged up into Charlie's nostrils. Snapping out of his shock, he urgently took a deep lungful of air. Seeing his reflection as clear as crystal in the shop window, he blew as hard as he could on the conch, and as he did, time came to a grinding halt. Everything went hazy. The most beautiful music filled the night; music that was like the sound of ocean waves breaking on the shore, like the sound of a thousand violins, like the sound of honeybees swarming on a summer's day. Whatever it was, it worked.

If you had been watching Charlie and Moon racing down the hill towards the ANIMALS-R-US emporium, on an oversized skateboard with two Thunder Eggs precariously attached, you would have been most surprised to see them carried through the window (without breaking it) by a man with a long white beard and a woman with a huge beehive hairdo. And when they sailed through the window, Charlie, Moon and the two Thunder Eggs completely disappeared.

Nano-seconds later, a surprised Charlie and Moon found themselves standing on the skateboard in a rather run down backyard. Somehow, the sound of the conch had transported them without harm through Weavel's windowpane in a time warp or another dimension. The boy and bird shook hands and claws and celebrated quietly. They were still alive, for the moment.

While Moon removed his parrot costume, Charlie looked around, checking out the surroundings. Behind them was a high wall with barbed wire and broken jagged glass along the top of it, one that even Charlie wouldn't dare climb. In front of them, the dark rear of a building reached towards the sky as if it was trying to escape. Stacked high against the walls and scattered around the yard was an enormous quantity of wooden crates, all wrenched open. Charlie wiped the dusty grime from one of them. There were some markings burnt into the wooden panels that read:

For Delivery to:
ANIMALS-R-US
Royal Blue and Gold Winged Eagles
Box No. 9

Charlie was shocked. These were the crates in which Moon and his family had been incarcerated and taken to the toymaker's dungeon to await their terrible fate. Their fate of being turned into stuffed toys. Charlie turned to Moon and the little eagle spoke to him in the saddest of tones.

"Yes, Charlie. This is Skunk Weavel's storage yard. Just over there is a flight of stairs that leads down to a deep cellar where the animals are kept prisoner until they are turned into toys. Hopefully, the hole that I escaped through is still there. I'll go down, climb in and open up the door so we can get the eggs in. I won't be long."

"But what are we going to do about Penelope?"

At that moment Moon didn't really care about Penelope. All he was interested in was saving his family. He crept along next to the wooden crates and disappeared down the stairs.

Charlie waited with bated breath. What if Moon was caught? What if the eagles had already been stuffed? And how had Penelope found ANIMALS-R-US before he had? And why was she there at all? He had seen her and Skunk laughing together. What was that about? Charlie refused to believe that his sister was in cahoots with the toymaker. The only reasonable possibility was that she was trapped inside, and Charlie would have to rescue her too. What a pain!

A strange noise disturbed Charlie's train of thought—a noise like the shuffling of a pack of cards. Charlie hid in the shadows behind one of the crates.

"Pssst." Charlie could hear someone. The sound came again. "Pssst. Pssst." Then a long coooooo-eeeeeee.

"Who is it? Who's there?" asked Charlie, frightened that he'd been discovered.

"It's us," said Snoozeball and Runningmouth. They stuck their heads up from the other side of the crate that Charlie was hiding behind.

"What are *you* two doing here? How did you get here?" whispered Charlie, hardly able to believe his eyes.

"Well, Penelope opened up the secret tunnel, and when we reached the end of it we found ourselves outside ANIMALS-R-US. We just thought you needed help and...err...those Snarlies won't be content unless we play a third game of Happy Families...just to let them know who's the best. You know how it is." Then came another *pssst*. This time, it was Moon. He had climbed in through the hole and opened the door to the cellar. He beckoned them to hurry. Immediately, Charlie and the two Thunder Egg Chickens pushed the skateboard to the back door where the little bird stood waiting. The chickens greeted Moon and, although Moon was a little surprised to see them, he welcomed the extra assistance. Together, they carefully lifted the eggs off the board and were just about to take them through the gap when they heard yet another *pssst*. Two familiar voices rang out through the night.

"Welcome to ANIMALS-R-US," they cackled. Giggling like a pair of naughty schoolboys, the Snarlies dropped a large net onto the group. As it fell on their heads and wrapped itself all around their bodies, gooba dripped from the webbing that entangled them. Out of the shadows stepped Flip and Flop, wearing wrap-around sunglasses and singing, "Nah-nah, nee-nah-nah. Who's a clever Snarlie? Who's a clever Snarlie? We are. We are." They gave each other high fives and laughed until oily tears ran down their beaks. A dejected Charlie sat down and stared at the ground. He'd lost his half of *The Book of Dreams* and now they were trapped in the yard. There seemed to be no way out.

"Won't Master Skunk be happy with us? One boy, a stinky eagle and two Thunder Egg Chickens to go," sang Flip. The gawping Snarlies dragged their four captives down to the dark cellar where the rest of the eagles were imprisoned. In the shadows, Flop took hold of Runningmouth, held her claw very gently and even managed to give her a kiss on the beak when Flip wasn't looking.

As they were pushed and shoved into the cold and dingy dungeon, Charlie was shocked by what he saw. In the dim light, a vanquished army of Blue and Gold Winged eagles was individually chained to the walls. Some of them had lost many feathers. Some had blood on their talons where they'd tried to wrench themselves free of their shackles. Some were slumped over in despair. But when the newcomers entered the eagles' prison, all of these magnificent birds, the bloodied and the broken-spirited, stood up as one and proudly welcomed their would-be rescuers. Charlie felt his heart begin to melt and his eyes become all watery. Both Snoozeball and Runningmouth, so moved by what they saw, took out their handkerchiefs and blew their beaks. A stronger-looking eagle spoke out when the Snarlies chained Charlie, Moon, Snoozeball and Runningmouth to the wall. It was Moon's father, Listen-To-The-Wind.

"Welcome back, Prince Golden Moon."

"Prince Golden Moon?" asked Charlie, eyes wide.

"Yeah. That's my real name," replied Moon. "Over the top, isn't it?" said the little eagle, slightly embarrassed. Listen-To-The-Wind continued,

"Welcome Charlie Ramsbottom and Thunder Egg Chickens. I am Listen-To-The-Wind, King of the Eagles, and this is my Queen, I-Can-See-For-Miles, and we are indebted to you forever, no matter what happens to us."

"Shut up, you stupid old eagle," snarled Flip. "Come on Flop, let's go and cook those Thunder Eggs. I'm feeling rather peckish. I bet they're really scrumptious and delicious. I could do with a large snack." Before Flip and Flop climbed up the cellar steps, Flop was able to give Runningmouth a quick loving glance. She fluttered her eyelids daintily back at him, hoping her cherished one would rescue her.

Listen-To-The-Wind spoke again. "Charlie Ramsbottom, Thunder Egg Chickens, I am grateful for your efforts. We are all grateful, but as you can see, we are chained, you are chained and there is nothing we can do. We will just have to accept our fate with all the dignity we can muster."

Charlie and Moon gave each other a knowing look. Moon spoke first. "Father, don't you notice something different about me?" His father looked at him, and so did his mother.

"Come to think of it, you do look different. You've grown, and by the looks of it you haven't had a wash since you left here."

"Father, Mother, look at my beak. Look at my beak! Those eggs that the Snarlies are going to cook are the key to our freedom," said Moon. Listen-To-The-Wind and I-Can-See-For-Miles looked puzzled. The rest of the eagle clan was also confused, but reveled in the bizz-buzz of excitement and anticipation that was gradually building. Moon continued, "Somehow, the yolk from the Thunder Eggs can return our noses into proper beaks. Look, look at mine." He turned his head around so the full circle of imprisoned eagles could see his new sharp beak. Amidst the excitement, I-Can-See-For-Miles addressed them all tearfully.

"My beautiful son, those eggs may be our salvation, but we're here and the eggs are upstairs cooking." All of a sudden Charlie had another of his cerebral surges.

"Listen," he said. "The eggs may be upstairs, but there are two of us here who can lay more, and I sure ain't one of them." He turned excitedly to Snoozeball and Runningmouth.

"Do you think you could lay an egg or two between you?" It was Snoozeball's turn to look a little sad as she spoke.

"We are too old to lay eggs now, Charlie. Our egg-laying days are done. We're only good for rice pudding, hot chocolate and..." As she stopped speaking, a glint appeared in her eye. "There is *one* thing that we're still good at though," she said.

"What's that?" asked Listen-To-The-Wind.

"Playing Happy Families, and I bet at least one of those Snarlies couldn't resist another game. Could he Runningmouth?" asked Snoozeball of her friend. Uncharacteristically, Runningmouth said nothing, but blushed furiously.

Moon quickly explained to the rest of the eagles about the Snarlies' weakness. Very soon, a jeering cry began to rise from the cellar.

"Snarlies can't play Families, Snarlies can't play Families, Snarlies can't play Families. Nah-nah, nee-nah-nah," went the chant.

Waiting for the eggs to boil, Flip and Flop pretended to ignore the call, but it really got to them. It snuck into their brains like the smell of fresh-sugared doughnuts. Unable to resist the taunt, they chimed out their own refrain, "Oh yes we ca-an, Oh yes we ca-an." But it was no use. The heckling from below tormented them so much that within no time at all, Flip and Flop were rushing down into the cellar to release Snoozeball and Runningmouth.

"O.K. you stupid chickens," drawled Flip. "We'll show you who can play. We'll show you who's the best." Flip and Flop led the two chickens upstairs to the storeroom where the table was cleared with one swoop of a wing.

"We've got to hurry with this game and we've got to be quiet," said Flip. "Skunk's just popped out for the moment," (or so they thought). "He's taken some stuffed polar bears to Weavel World for the big opening. If he comes back and sees us playing Happy Families, he'll go crazy."

"O.K. let's get on with this game so we can thrash you to bits," said Snoozeball.

"Yeah, let's get on, let's get on. Who's afraid of a silly old toymaker?" chimed in Runningmouth boldly, although she kept looking over her shoulder to make sure she was safe. The Thunder Egg Chickens and Snarlies sat down, ready to lay their cards on the table. Snoozeball and Runningmouth eyed the stove behind Flip and Flop. The Thunder Eggs were on the boil. Next to the eggs was a large pot that bubbled with a disgusting looking brown mixture. It had the following words written on it:

The Secret of Life

The next stage of the plan was about to go into action, but first things first. Runningmouth shuffled the cards in her inimitable fashion and exchanged secret loving smiles with her beau. There was an oppressive hush in the room, broken only by the persistent oozing sounds and the relentless squidging-widging noise of the elixir on the stove. The rattle of the Thunder Eggs wobbling around in the boiling water also filled the subversive silence to the extent that you had to listen carefully to hear the hush at all!

Flip was just about to call a hand when they heard an unusual noise slowly moving down the corridor to the room where they were seated. It sounded like someone badly singing an operatic aria, while someone else was laughing at the same time. Doors were being slammed and then reopened. Occasionally, the high-pitched singing became completely unbearable.

"That wailing," said Snoozeball, "is worse than your singing, Flip, and that's saying something." Runningmouth couldn't resist adding her piece of rapier-like wit either. "You've heard of the voice that launched a thousand ships," she said. "Well, that must be the voice that sunk them." For a moment the four birds were as one, and all broke into laughter as the voice struggled to reach the incredibly high soprano part from *The Queen of the Night.*

Down in the dungeon below, Charlie and the eagles heard the noise too. From the sound of the awful high-pitched, out-of-tune notes, Charlie knew it could be none other than Penelope. In a panic, he tried to wrestle free of his chains, but it was useless. Upstairs, Skunk was encouraging Penelope to keep singing as he steered her towards a door.

"This way my dear. I think your brother will be here very soon and then we can both show him what a clever girl you are!"

From the card table, the Snarlies and the Chickens watched the handle of the door begin to turn slowly, creaking like they do in extremely scary movies. At that moment, Penelope let out a high operatic C, which started cracking the glasses in the storeroom. When the door finally opened, Skunk gestured for Penelope to enter the room that was not a storeroom at all, but actually a laboratory. The Snarlies and the Thunder Egg Chickens froze. Flip went red in the face, suddenly realizing who it was.

"It's the master! Oh my gooba! What's he going to do to us?" he whispered frantically to the others. There was nowhere to run. There was nowhere to hide. They would have to face the music, Penelope's music!

Chapter Thirteen: This Is No Yolk

Skunk Weavel followed Penelope into the laboratory, feigning wonder and awe at her caterwaulling rendition of *The Queen of the Night*. The Snarlies and the Chickens, though petrified of the Toyminator, had to cover their ears to try to block out Penelope's screeching. Snoozeball and Runningmouth practically laid eggs at the sight of Skunk Weavel, and the Snarlies literally shook when they saw their evil master.

"Come, my dear girl, come over here and give this a stir," said Skunk, pointing to the bubbling cauldron marked *The Secret of Life*. Penelope did as she was told, looking to Skunk Weavel for approval. "I've always wanted an assistant of your calibre, of your towering intellect, your brain power." Proud of her new-found status, Penelope smiled a smile so wide, that if it had been any wider, her teeth would have fallen out of their gummy sockets.

Locking the door and slowly gazing around the room, the master manipulator licked his lips and flashed a crooked set of yellowing fangs at the Thunder Egg Chickens when he saw the eggs a-boiling. Then ever so slowly he cast a dark glare at the table. The two Snarlies slid into their seats pretending to be innocent, trying to hopelessly hide the grimy deck of playing cards. The blood drained from Skunk's body, his face blanched to a whiter shade of white, and just for a moment you could almost hear the earth groan, so sinister was his gaze. But Skunk had a deadline. In no time at all, he had a grip on the situation. His tongue slid in and slimed out from his purple lips. A slight trembling movement crept from the corner of his mouth, allowing a smirk to slowly light up his face. What a happy little toymaker he was. Very deliberately, he reached into his left pocket and with a great flourish, pulled out the newly acquired half of *The Book*. Dipping into his other pocket, he pulled out the second half of the *The Book*. Holding the two parts high in the air, he waited. And then, with the attraction of a magnet, the two halves joined, causing the lights overhead to flicker madly. Skunk gleefully waved the new book for everyone to see. The title now read, *The Book of Skunk Weavel Rules.*

"This book...this book," he exclaimed, excited as a rotten piece of pumpkin. He caressed the jeweled edges of the book, "This magic book will make me the most powerful man in the City of the Quincequonces, in the world, in the whole universe. My new empire begins tomorrow with the sweet ka-ching of thousands of cash registers ringing. Stupid people will line up to receive an extremely overpriced stuffed eagle from my new empire in Weavel World. Perhaps they'll even want to buy plush Thunder Egg Chickens." He broke into a cackle that was worse than fingernails being driven across a chalkboard. Flip saw his chance for a reprieve from his master and added to the celebratory mood.

"Sir Skunk, Lord Weavel or may I call you Your Highness?" He continued smarmily, "Not only will you sell stuffed cuddly eagles and two Thunder Egg Chickens but, methinks..." he leaned in close to his master's ear and whispered, "Would not the potion also work on this sweet Ramsbottom girl and her charming brother, Master Charles?" Flip smiled an 'aren't-I-the-clever-one' smile and Skunk grinned to himself and licked his lips. The thought of making children into cuddly toys had not occurred to him before, but he immediately knew its sales potential. There would be buyers from all over the world for this kind of product, buyers who believed children should be seen and not heard. And how better to turn that saying into a reality! Toy kids! Who knew where that could lead?

"Of course, Bird-Brain One. You are so right." Skunk turned to Penelope and said with a fake smile, "Tell me my dear, how is the consistency of my elixir?"

"I got rid of all the lumps. It's really smooth and creamy now."

"Perhaps we should let your brother try some. What do you think?"

Penelope's face turned a shade of red, her ire arising. "*I* want to try it first. It's not fair!"

"Oh no, my dear. The second spoonful is always better." Penelope calmed down and gloated at her importance.

Taking Flip to one side, Skunk whispered, "Bring the little urchin to me. I'll try the potion on him first, and his asinine sister can watch. If it works on little boys, then she can have a tasteroni too. And then, yes then, maybe we can get rid of all those other despicable children who come in here with their useless parents and pester me for silly cheap toys. Now, take these ridiculous overgrown chickens downstairs, chain them up and bring me the Ramsbottom kid."

Flip and Flop bustled Snoozeball and Runningmouth down the cellar stairs. While Flip was chaining Snoozeball, Flop delicately placed the shackles around Runningmouth's ankles.

"I'm so sorry, my darling. I have no choice," he whispered with a tear rolling down his snout.

When the Snarlies unshackled Charlie, all the eagles complained vociferously, but they were too weak to do anything to prevent him from being taken. Skunk had even clipped their wings so they couldn't fly. Flip and Flop frogmarched Charlie up the cellar stairs and pushed him through the door. Nearly stumbling, Charlie entered the room and looked around. There was his horrid sister stirring a pot of Skunk's killer liquid. Was she stupid or just a complete and total airhead? Charlie stared at Penelope in disbelief. She raised her eyebrows at Charlie's show of disdain and laughed to herself as if she had cracked a private joke. Then she flipped her hair and turned away, continuing to stir the pot.

Laying his eyes on the toymaker, Charlie was surprised to see how hideous the evil one really was—greasy hair, food-stained coat, long, dirty fingernails. And when the Skunk smiled, exposing his set of dingy misshapen teeth, Charlie shuddered and his skin crawled. In a flash, he recalled the number of times Weavel had tried to enter his mind and brainwash him.

"Sit down!" hissed the demented subjugator, spraying Charlie's face with a mist of spit.

The Snarlies pushed Charlie into a metal chair and started to saunter away. Skunk looked incredulously at his thugs and growled, "You two sit in those chairs and guard him." The two Snarlies sheepishly sat down on either side of the prisoner.

Skunk leaned down and pushed his face as close as he could to Charlie's; so close that Charlie could feel the moisture from the toymaker's putrid breath. He almost passed out from the reek of the impacted food, rotting in his mouth.

"Look what I've got. What you so stupidly gave me," said Weavel, holding up *The Book of Skunk Weavel Rules*.

"Now I am in control. I will erase all drea...drea." But he couldn't say "dreams" because it would bring him out in a cold sweat. Without warning, Skunk pushed a button and clamps sprang out from all three chairs, locking in a tangle of arms and legs, completely entrapping them all!

"Deadly," shouted Penelope, her eyes almost shooting out of her head. "Just like a horror movie!"

"Thank you Bird-Brain One and Bird-Brain Two. Not only will we have a stuffed boy, chickens and eagles, but two stuffed Snarlies as well." Insidiously, he spun around on his greasy feet and smiled at Penelope. "And you, my faithful assistant, will help me." His heinous laugh filled the room. Flip and Flop were so enraged, they tried to shoot a stream of hot gooba at Skunk, but he had their measure and swiftly taped over their gooba holes. The Snarlies realized their predicament and started begging for their sorry lives. "But aren't we a vital part of ANIMALS-R-US?" moaned Flip.

"That's a joke," laughed the Toyminator. He pointed to a large flat-screen television that showed the front of the shop. Then he pushed a button, the flashy signage displaying ANIMALS-R-US. Another push revealed the real sign, the additional letters E...L...E...S...S... coming into view. Flip and Flop looked confused. "Get it, you sniveling excuses for dog's breath?!" snorted Skunk Weavel. "ANIMALS-R-USELESS! And kids are useless too!" he shouted, cackling insanely.

"Yeah, kids are useless too!" shouted Penelope, completely under Skunk's spell.

All the while, Charlie watched, helpless.

"You'll never get away with this, Skunk, you...you...you rotter!" shouted Charlie.

"Shut your trap, snivel snot," said Skunk.

"Yeah, shut up, snivel snot," echoed Penelope again, relishing her role as Skunk's faithful assistant and energetically stirring the potion that was bubbling and spitting on the stove.

The Thunder Eggs were also on the stove, and at that precise moment they were boiled to perfection, their yolks just as Skunk liked them, runny and slimy. Skunk turned off the gas. With an enormous set of rusty tongs, he placed the eggs into two large bowls and put them on the table opposite Charlie and the Snarlies. Sitting down on his throne-like seat, he caressed his lips with that awful tongue. Very carefully, he lopped the top off one of the Thunder Eggs and stuck a piece of mouldy bread into its golden yolk. The goo from the Thunder Egg yolk dribbled down the side of the eggshell, totally mesmerizing Skunk by the copious amount of free food. Watching on like a drooling dog, Penelope licked her lips and continued to stir the pot.

Skunk opened *The Book of Skunk Weavel Rules* and began reading and eating at the same time, his mouth like an open washing machine while he smacked his lips and sucked in the egg yolk off the stale bread—truly a horrible sight.

"Look, boy. Look," he said, spitting goo into Charlie's face, hair and ears. He shoved the book in front of Charlie's nose. Charlie was even more dismayed when he read the caption:

**As Skunk Weavel ate one of the Thunder Eggs,
the Secret of Life
had nearly finished cooking.
The next thing for Skunk Weavel to do was to
pour the elixir down
Charlie Ramsbottom's throat.**

Charlie pretended to cry, all the time thinking of a way that he could break free and attack Skunk. As for his sister, it was unbelievable! She stood there like a groupie, watching Skunk in adoration. But as the evil genius dug into one of the eggs like a human bulldozer, Charlie happened to glance down at the floor. Through the cracks in the dusty floorboards, he could see the vague outline of the eagles chained to the dungeon walls. If he could get the egg yolk to spill through the flooring to the birds down below, maybe they could eat the yolk and then rise up against the corrupted toymaker.

Charlie whispered to the Snarlies amidst Skunk's awful

slurping noise.

"Pssst, listen you two. If we can get that table to shake, rattle and roll, perhaps one of the Thunder Eggs might fall off and spill through the floor."

"Don't be so stu-," Flip started, until he happened to glance down at the floor. Through the cracks in the dusty floorboards, he could also see the vague outline of the eagles chained to the dungeon walls. Yes, the egg yolk *could* spill through the flooring, but whether the birds down below would notice and whether they would eat the yolk was just a chance they would all have to take.

"O.K. pardner. How do we go about this?" whispered Flip to Charlie.

"I'll create a diversion while you and Flop kick the legs of the table."

Suddenly, Skunk's telephone clanged from inside the shop. Standing up from the table, he slithered out of the room to take the call.

When Skunk had gone, Charlie looked at his sister stirring the pot and said with mocking sweetness, "I say, P, could you show us how clever you are and sing your twenty-seven multiplication times table? I'm sure you've aced it by now, and it sounds so good with your Mozartian variation."

Penelope puffed up a little. She couldn't help herself, and began reciting her twenty-seven times-table in true operatic style. It was the most horrid rendition of a multiplication table ever heard before. In fact, it was so high in pitch and so completely out of tune that paint began peeling off the walls.

Although his sister had been lost to the dark side and still couldn't sing to save her life, Charlie was amazed to say the least. Penelope had finally mastered her twenty-seven times table. What a brain box!

"Once twenty-seven is twenty-seven. Two twenty-sevens are fifty four..." sang the deranged Penelope. All of a sudden, Skunk burst back into the room and stared at Penelope in disbelief.

"Would you be quiet," he said, getting annoyed with his protégé. "I'm trying to take an important phone call." But nothing could stop Penelope. She was on a roll and continued crooning. Completely irritated by Penelope's grating fortissimo, Skunk grabbed a piece of mouldy bread and shoved it into her mouth.

Charlie whispered to Flip, "When he's gone, kick the table over, if you can."

"What did he say?" blurted out Flop. Flip started to reach out with his leg towards the table to show Flop.

"I said kick the table over," Charlie whispered again as Skunk checked the potion.

"What are you two up to?" he spat at the Snarlies.

"They're savoring the smell of your delicious elixir, sir," replied Charlie sarcastically, managing to stop the Snarlies shuffling before the evil toymaker saw what they were doing. Skunk raised his eyebrows as if to say, "silly boy," and then left the room to finish his call. But Charlie wasn't so silly. He called on Penelope's vanity once more as she bravely swallowed the musty bread in one gagging gulp, only to continue her operatic twenty-seven times table.

"Six times twenty-seven is one hundred and sixty two," she sang proudly as she stirred the pot, waving her spoon like a conductress, bits of the concoction landing on the floor. "Hey, watch what you're doing!" Skunk bellowed as he came back into the room. He sat down and continued glutting himself on the egg, trying to ignore Penelope's seemingly futile and inharmonious rendering of her mathematical melody. Oh, how he would have liked to gag her and tie her up with the rest, but he had plans for the irritating girl.

This time both Snarlies and Charlie reached out with their feet. They could just about touch the legs of the table.

Charlie whispered to Flip, "You countdown from three, then we all kick the table as hard as we can." Flip started counting very proudly in his best operatic baritone singing voice, as if in competition with Penelope.

"Three - two - four - five..."

"What are you doing?" said Charlie in hushed but urgent tones.

"I'm counting. I'm counting," whispered Flip back to Charlie, the numbers in Penelope's song completely confusing him.

"But you're going up instead of down," replied Charlie, rather impatiently. "And why are you singing?"

"Now, don't tell me how to count, young pardner. I'll have you know, I was at the top of my class in counting. And don't tell me how to sing, neither. I'm just as good as your sister. In fact, I can recite the thirty times table in the deepest tones you've ever heard." With that, Flip, alias Don Gi-Snarlie, sang the first line of the thirty times table just to prove that he could do it. In a booming voice, he began: "Once thirty is forty. See! So there!"

"What are you up to, Flip?" said Skunk, annoyed by the unbalanced operatic duet. At the same time, a call came across his two-way radio.

"I was just adding up how many animals are going to be stuffed, Master," said Flip, quickly covering his tracks.

"Well, do it quietly if you have to, you crusty piece of craddit's breath," said Skunk, sliding out of the room to take his call. Flip began again, whispering into Charlie's ear ever so softly. Skunk could be heard outside the door talking to someone on the other end of the line, "Yes, and make sure the stuffed polar bears are in position. Beats me why everyone loves them!"

"Three, four, two, five...." Charlie guessed by Flip's method of counting that the next number might possibly be the number one but the bird took ever such a long time to reach the same conclusion. He must have gone through it half a dozen times before Charlie saw the Snarlie's face light up and his lips begin to say the magic number. Flip's eyes were full of pride as the numbers rolled off his tongue. "Three, four, two, five, ONE!"

Then together, Flip and Flop and Charlie lashed out at the table legs. The table shook violently, and Charlie and the Snarlies watched in suspense as the Thunder Eggs began to topple. Just as they were about to fall towards the floor, Skunk raced into the room, made a lunge for the eggs, and saved them.

However, Skunk was not prepared for Penelope's finale. She hit a note in her operatic multiplication-times table aria that can only be described as the shrillest note ever heard by anyone and one that has never been heard or reached again. The note cracked the eggshells into thousands of pieces. The yolk gushed out from the split eggs like water exploding through a dam wall, pouring down through the cracks in the floorboards.

"You are an amazing girl," said Skunk sardonically. "Get me a glass of the elixir. The time has come," smiled the toymaker, hiding his contempt for Penelope. She quickly scooped some of the liquid into a container and grovelingly handed it to her new master.

"Say hello to your new world, Ramsbottom," Skunk hissed in Charlie's face. "It's time for you to experience *The Secret of Life*."

"Just like a horror film. Wicked. Sick!" Penelope sang out.

"And you will be next if you're good," he shouted, his veins protruding from his neck like mouldy string beans. Then he moved in closer so that he and Charlie were eye to eye. Smiling savagely and whispering in a voice that was strangely calm, so that only Charlie could hear, he said, "Think your last thought kid, take your last breath, because the Secret of Life is…death!"

"My name is not *kid*," said Charlie forcefully. "It's Charlie Ramsbottom, and you'd be wise to stop what you're doing, otherwise Bizz-Buzz will come and he'll…he'll…" said Charlie playing for some extra time so the Thunder Egg yolk could take its effect down in the dungeon.

"Bizz-Buzz? He's a phony, a namby pamby. You're wasting your time." Skunk went on and on about how stupid Bizz-Buzz was, which was exactly what Charlie was hoping he would do.

Down below in the cellar, Snoozeball and Runningmouth felt something dripping onto their heads, their claws still in their ears, Penelope's last note still reverberating painfully. It was Thunder Egg yolk. Moon noticed it as well. He could smell its delicious aroma. It was dripping all around them like honey from the gods. Moon told the eagles to drink as much as they could and they all dipped their noses into the golden elixir, from every crack and crevasse. In no time at all, a whole army of straight-nosed beaks turned into real eagle beaks! The owners of these new razor beaks instantly regained their strength, ripped free of their chains, then released Snoozeball and Runningmouth.

Upstairs, and completely unaware of what was happening in the cellar, Skunk was prattling on about Bizz-Buzz's failings so much that he didn't hear the eagles and chickens down below perched on each other's shoulders, cutting escape holes with their new sharp beaks into the cellar ceiling leading to the store.

"Now, scoop up every little bit of the yolk and hold it in your beaks until I give the word!" ordered Listen-To-The-Wind.

When they were all assembled in the shop front, the King signaled. Quickly, the eagles went along the shelves pouring the Thunder Egg yolk from their beaks into the concretized mouths of the stuffed koala bears, flamingos, chipmunks, tree kangaroos, penguins, squirrels, wombats, cheetahs, Tasmanian tigers, elephants, iguanas, snow leopards, bandicoots, pandas, jaguars, polar bears, gorillas and the teddy bears. Skunk didn't know it, but in his own warehouse a multitude of winged assailants, ground troops and underground foragers were assembling, waiting to arrest him. The animals had to be patient and careful because Charlie was still captive. Very quietly, they broke through the many doors that separated them from the toymaker and his prisoners. They finally reached the last door. Carefully, Listen-To-The-Wind turned the handle, but Skunk had double locked it from the other side.

Inside the laboratory, Skunk was directing Penelope. "Now give your brother the drink and he will discover *The Secret of Life.*"

"Why can't I try it first?" moaned Penelope.

"Remember what we said: second scoop is best!" Penelope smiled gleefully and held Charlie's head back.

"Please, Penelope," cried Charlie. "He's tricking you. You're making a big mistake. You're gonna…" But Penelope clamped a hand over her brother's mouth and cut him off. The Snarlies sat there frozen in terror. Their turn was next!

"There you go again, Creepoid," said Penelope. "Always thinking you know better than your big sister. Now stay still and open wide." Charlie struggled, clamping his mouth shut, but Penelope, with the strength of an orangutan, pried it open.

Outside the laboratory in the hallway, the animals suddenly saw the electricity go on and off. A shudder ran through the building shaking the foundations. Dust fell from the ceiling creating a sooty mist. An icy chill pervaded the atmosphere. They were too late. Sir Edward Bainbridge, leader of the teddy bears, was the first to speak.

"I'm afwaid to say it chaps, but my pwopensity for sniffing out danger tells me that Skunk Weavel has poured that evil potion down young Charlie Wamsbottom's thwoat," he uttered dejectedly as he whiffed the air around him.

"NO!" every animal cried in unison at this horrible turn of events.

Inside the storeroom, Skunk and Penelope watched Charlie turn into a humanized stuffed toy. His eyes doubled in size. His eyelashes thickened and his hair shot up like it had been electrified. A permanent smile appeared on his face and his clothes became fluffy and cuddly.

"Perfect! Who would have thought it?" The Toyminator was very proud of himself.

"Oh look at him! He's so cute now," said Penelope. "I could put him on the end of my bed. If only he was like this all of the time."

"Young Ramsbottom's sister, what a wonderful assistant you have turned out to be. Now you'll have the privilege of watching the King of the Eagles become a cuddly toy," said Skunk.

"Wicked. How long does the potion actually last, Mr. Weavel?" Penelope asked, sucking up to the toymaker. Skunk turned and looked deep into Penelope's soul.

"Forever," he hissed.

The blood drained from Penelope's body sending her straight into shock.

Oblivious to Penelope's distress, Skunk went to the basement door. When he opened it and went down the stairs to grab the king, he stood there stupidly for a moment, looking at the empty shackles lying on the floor. A large guttural yowl issued from his lips. Instantly, all his basic slimy survival instincts told him that trouble was just around the corner. Well actually, in the next room.

Hurrying back into the lab, Skunk grabbed *The Book* and a dusty bottle of the potion from off a greasy shelf. He was about to make a run for it when he had what was for him, a wonderful idea. He grabbed Penelope, who was standing stock still, her face an unearthly white, comprehending the enormity of what she had done. Without wasting a beat, Skunk flung the catatonic Penelope over his shoulder and opened the back door to the storage yard. No one would ever attack him while he had the Ramsbottom girl. With her as his prisoner, he would be able to hold out till midnight, *The Book* would become completely his and he would be all-powerful.

Escaping by the narrowest of margins, Skunk shoved Penelope into the back seat of an old Jaguar sports car next to two gigantic fluffy polar bears. He jumped into the front and started up the motor just as the animals broke the lock and burst through the door into the storeroom.

The sight that greeted the group was indeed a sad one. Leaning over in a chair was Charlie Ramsbottom, their hero— stuffed. The Snarlies were absolutely terrified. They quaked in their boots for fear of retribution by the eagles and the menagerie.

While Skunk's sports car could be heard roaring off into the distance, Moon picked up an old can in his beak and flew down to the cellar to scoop some yolk into it. Quickly returning, he sat on Charlie's shoulder, and with the help of his mother and father, prized open his friend's mouth.

"Drink this yolk, Charlie," Moon whispered sadly. "It will

unfreeze you. It's got to. It's our only chance." He poured a little into Charlie's mouth but Charlie didn't move. So he tipped some more of the yolk down Charlie's rigid throat. Still nothing happened. Finally, he poured in the remainder. Snoozeball gloomily said that all they could do was watch for the yolk to take effect, if it had any effect at all. The animals waited and waited for what seemed like hours.

When Penelope poured the deadly elixir down Charlie's throat, Charlie had drifted out of his body and now watched helplessly from above as the crowd tried to bring him back. He felt himself slipping further away, away from his physical shell as he traveled down a tunnel towards a bright light. In the blink of an eye, he found himself standing, looking at his parent's house. Then in a flash, he was inside the kitchen watching his mum and dad. They were sitting at the table leafing through a photograph album of him and Penelope. Both parents looked very sad. Charlie looked up. Bizz-Buzz and Doreen Tremblingknees were watching him watch his parents. It felt as if they were looking deep into his heart. Bizz-Buzz spoke to him but his words were as thought and not spoken.

"Charlie Ramsbottom, your time has come. Now you must choose what you want. You can keep drifting into the other worlds, or you can stand up and take on this reptilian brother of mine and show him who you truly are. You can save the eagles and all the other creatures and restore *The Book of Dreams* to its rightful place."

At that moment, Charlie's skin became unbearable itchy. Bizz-Buzz's thoughts came through to him again.

"Charlie. Think back to what you saw in *The Book of Dreams;* the young boy trying to stop the Snarlies from taking *The Book* from the old man."

Charlie answered in thought, "How do you know about that?" Then it dawned on him. "That boy was *me* and *you* were the old man?"

Bizz-Buzz nodded, "That's right Charlie, you were choosing your birthday gift but we were interrupted. That is why you were chosen to take on this task. You have to finish the dream. Since you started your journey, you have become an Eagle Spirit. In fact, if the eagles die, so will you. You of all people now understand their plight." Charlie responded in thought. "I don't want to die. I just want to have a happy birthday and go back to what was." Bizz-Buzz continued.

"What was is no longer."

Charlie watched his parents cuddle into each other more tightly.

"They look so sad."

"That's because they love you and Penelope and feel responsible for all that has happened."

"What can I do?"

"Take the next step and become the huge Eagle Spirit that you are."

"Tell me what I must do," said Charlie.

"Have a pure heart, know who you are and see yourself succeeding. It is never easy crossing the bridge, but you can always call on the Great Eagle Spirits to assist you."

Bizz-Buzz and Doreen Tremblingknees disappeared, and

Charlie felt himself rushing back to his body. It was Runningmouth who saw the first signs of life in Charlie. She screamed so loudly when Charlie moved that all of the animals jumped.

"The boy! The boy! I saw him move. I saw him move. The boy, the boy! I saw him move I say. I saw him move. The..." Snoozeball put a wing around Runningmouth to comfort her and said, "We understand, Runningmouth. We understand." Obviously, the adventure was starting to take its toll on everyone.

"But I did! Look!"

Encouraged by the gathering, Charlie was gradually able to bring the life back into his frozen limbs. It took nearly an hour for him to come fully around. First, a wind streamed in through the area just above the bridge of his nose. His eyes twitched and his body jolted. Then his fingers and arms started to dance and itch. His legs kicked up and down like a stomping horse. He blew air across his lips. His head started to shake and his ears flapped. And all of the time, he was calling out words from the other worlds. Finally, he raised his fist and punched it high into the air to stand up again, alive and ready for action. Everyone cheered and clapped. He was back! Moon cried out the loudest when he saw his friend return to the land of the living. And when the eagles recognized Charlie's new spirit, his Eagle Spirit, their own spirits soared. They spread their wings and bowed in reverence as Listen-To-The-Wind welcomed him in the old Eaglish language.

"Sompa soo sompa, spiritoo, moo hompa," said the eagle king. Charlie inwardly knew this meant, "Welcome Great Eagle Spirit so brave." All the other eagles repeated Listen-To-The-

Wind's refrain, flapped their wings and bowed their heads in reverence. Behind the Eagle king's back, Moon gave Charlie a high five.

Without further delay, a plan was hatched. The most important thing was to rescue Penelope, traitor though she was. Then the book had to be retrieved to stop Skunk Weavel from taking control of the dreaming world. The trouble was they didn't know where the cruel toymaker had gone. The eagles decided to send a reconnaissance team to look for that nasty excuse for a human being. With Charlie in the lead, the team of eagles all eagle-hopped into the yard and started to try to fly but it was no use. Their wings had been clipped. The Thunder Egg yolk had only restored their strength and bent their beaks into the correct shape; it couldn't make them fly immediately.

Charlie took control of the situation. "We'll have to find some other way. Wait here." He rushed back into the storeroom and returned with Flip and Flop who were whimpering and crying. Everyone groaned. Charlie silenced them, "Listen, they're with us. Honest! They want revenge. Skunk Weavel blackmailed them to do his dirty work. He bribed them and lied to them," shouted Charlie. "They know where he is! He's gone to Weavel World. Please. Please. Animal to animal, make them welcome."

Snoozeball stepped forward. She stood in front of Flip and Flop and looked them right in the eyes. "Apart from my learned friend and me, you two are the best darned Happy Family card players I've ever come across. I welcome you to our side." Then Runningmouth hopped forward.

"Yes, I'll say that again. I'll say that again. And I was never really frightened of you. I was just pretending. Believe me," she said as she looked at Flop with the softest of eyes. All the animals laughed. Listen-To-The-Wind stepped between the two Thunder Egg chickens and welcomed Flip and Flop to the group. Eagle upon eagle shook the Snarlie's claws and as they did, they all sensed a new kinship. When Moon and Charlie finally held the Snarlie's talons aloft in a victory salute, Flip and Flop were so moved by the whole experience that they cried and snotted on each other's shoulders. With their faces relaxed, they even started to actually look somewhat handsome. Well, as handsome as vultures could ever look!

"Follow me," shouted Charlie as he ran up the hill to the main road. Our young hero stood at the top of the crest, put two fingers in his mouth and gave a long whistle. From around the corner of the road came the sound of a bus. It was the No. 9 and right on time. As the red vehicle slowed, Doreen Tremblingknees looked as if she was dancing a waltz. She was. Charlie and the animals ran alongside the bus.

"I knew you'd come, I knew you'd come," said Charlie, puffing a little. "Have you got room for a band of koala bears, flamingos, chipmunks, tree kangaroos, penguins, squirrels, wombats, cheetahs, Tasmanian tigers, iguanas, snow leopards, bandicoots, pandas, jaguars, polar bears, gorillas and teddy bears?"

Doreen looked at the elephants askance and Charlie said, "Don't worry, the elephants can run alongside. All right lads?"

The elephants raised their trunks in agreement and Doreen

broke into a slow "let's twist again like we did last summer" dance, and said, "Yes, yes, yes." All the animals ran and hopped and jumped onto the bus.

"Where to, Charlie Ramsbottom?" she said excitedly. She was really going for it now as she sped up her twisty dance, the bus mimicking her movements at rocket speed.

"Weavel World and step on it, driver! We've only got about one hundred eagle hops left to rescue Penelope and save *The Book of Dreams* from falling into oblivion." Just as the words trailed out of Charlie's mouth, the most horrific thing happened. A sizzling electrical storm reared from out of nowhere and threw itself down upon the bus with all the fury of a gobful of goblins. Having engineered this masterstroke, Skunk Weavel was preparing to make his final move and wasn't going to give in. Quite the contrary, he was preparing for a victory. If he made it through until the next day, he would open Weavel World and many of the animals already poisoned by his evil brew would become extinct. Realizing the power of the storm, Listen-To-The-Wind knew he had to act quickly.

"Charlie Ramsbottom. You'll have to help get me onto the top of the bus. And you'll have to do it now!" Charlie looked outside as blackened hailstones hammered dents into the body of the red vehicle. There was no time to lose. He pulled down a window.

Listen-To-The-Wind climbed onto Charlie's back and spread his wings to protect his friend. To Charlie's astonishment, talons appeared at the end of his fingers. With his new found strength, he clawed his way slowly out of the small opening, up the side of the red double-decker bus, and onto its roof.

With hail and rain attacking his body, Charlie clung on for dear life. Gripping the top of the bus, he watched Listen-To-The-Wind move into an ancient dance ritual. The King seemed hypnotized, eagle-hopping in a full circle, nine times, almost dancing off the bus' roof each time he neared the edge.

The great bird gradually moved to the center of the circle, unfurled his enormous wings, braced himself against the elements and let out a long, haunting cry. Immediately, there was a remarkable response. It was like the beating of wings of the most enormous bird. From over the tops of the sky scraping buildings of the City of the Quincequonces, all species of birds began to descend upon the bus. Battalion upon battalion lined up in formation to protect the vehicle and escort it to Weavel World. With the arrival of so many birds, the storm subsided. Skunk Weavel's attack had been beaten off.

Now they were moving to the final phase of the quest: the showdown with the most evil Toyminator in the world.

Chapter Fourteen: The Great Awakening

Anyone who was asleep in bed that night in the City of the Quincequonces and who got up to look at the storm raging outside their window might have thought they were dreaming. They would have seen a red double-decker bus full of animals—without a bus driver—motoring past their house through the deserted city streets, flanked by a herd of elephants. And the bus, which had just been attacked by gangs of rain gremlins, was being followed and protected by squadron after squadron of starlings, crows, magpies, cuckoos, robins, multi-colored parrots, ospreys, owls, pelicans, cormorants, ravens, geese, condors, hawks, kookaburras, swallows, seagulls and every possible variety of bird that had the capability for flight.

Inside the bus, there was an air of excitement and anticipation. The animals were going to nail that toymaker once and for all. Flip and Flop were so overjoyed to be given the chance to avenge Skunk Weavel that they broke into song:

**"We are the creatures, yes we're great and small
Gonna stop Weavel, stop him once and for all…"**

Snoozeball and Runningmouth joined them in a quartet and by the hand of some unseen choral director, the whole busload of animals began singing. The birds flying protectively above the vehicle began whistling, chirping, tweeting, cawing, whippoorwilling, squawking, peeping and cheeping, all in the most glorious harmony. It was astonishing. The words became a battle cry to lift everyone's spirits.

'Cos we-e-e-e-e,
Cos we-e-e-e
We are a family,
And we know what we're worth!
'Cos we-e-e-e-e,
Oh we-e-e-e
We are united
And we're saving the earth.

Amidst the charged atmosphere, Charlie calculated that they would reach their destination with only minutes to spare. The time flew by and it wasn't long before the bus slowed down in front of Weavel World.

"Thank you, Doreen Tremblingknees," said Charlie.

"It's the least I could do, Charlie Ramsbottom, you brave boy," she replied. He kissed Doreen's hand as the animals bounded off the bus.

While Charlie was wishing Doreen farewell, Listen-To-The-Wind instructed his winged commanders to go and awaken every child in the City of the Quincequonces. They were to bring as many of the children as possible to Weavel World so they could witness the unraveling of the evil Weavel. The remainder of the Eagle Air Force immediately set out to Thunder Egg Farm to collect more life-saving Thunder Eggs so they could return to release their animal kin. As soon as the bus and flock after flock of birds disappeared into the night, Listen-To-The-Wind joined Charlie and the rest of the animal forces. They had just started to scale the walls of Weavel World, when Skunk began a series of attacks to stop them from reaching him before midnight.

The voices from The Plains of Desire were ordered to take up the first wave, their maddening and enticing whispers arising out of the sewers of the City,

**"...quincequonceeeee... eeeeat...
the...quincequoncee...quincequonceeeee...
eeeeat...the ...quincequoncee..."**

The incantation grew louder and louder until it surrounded the animals like a ring of fire. Within the nefarious circle, a multitude of skeletal hands rose up and tried to grab Charlie. Springing into action, the teddy bears stood shoulder to shoulder with the gorillas to smash the ghostly hands, while the polar bears created an icy cyclone that blew the deathly whisperers back to the Plains forever and a day.

As soon as that attack was thwarted, Skunk ordered the next wave. From the nearby streets, Charlie and his team heard a heavy grating noise, worse than a dentist's drill, and the sound of steel crunching against the tarmac of the road. The horrendous reverberation drew nearer. And then it was upon them. Bearing down the road towards the group, came an army of robots. Having marched from Skunk's factory, they halted and formed two long militaristic rows. In rotation, each line spat huge streams of steaming black slime from their metallic mouths at Charlie and his posse. Everyone dropped down to avoid being hit by the gunk, which burnt smoldering holes into the sidewalk as it hit the concrete. Thunderbolts of fire followed the slime, creating an intense heat that singed Charlie's eyebrows. The elephants began trumpeting defiantly at the robots and then dipping their trunks into a nearby storm-water drain, they raised themselves up on their back legs and shot water at the mean machines, drenching them in torrents. As the robots backed off, they counter-attacked, shooting off the most delicious tasting Quincequonce fruit at the group.

"Don't touch it!" shouted Charlie above the roar of the animals who hadn't eaten in days. The smell was so enticing that they had to hold each other's mouths shut to stop themselves from falling under the spell of the diabolical fruit. But the robots had one more trick up their rusting sleeves. They started to eat the quincequonces themselves and turned on Charlie and his friends, firing off round after round of stinky blasts of Ferocious Attacks of the Roaring Trumpets. Amidst the odorous odor, Charlie, holding his nose, called on Flip and Flop.

"Snarlies! Now's the time to redeem yourselves. See if you can stop those robots with a net of gooba, otherwise we'll all be suffocated by their gas."

"We're on the case, pardner," shouted Flip heroically. Flop turned and winked at Runningmouth, who whispered in her loved one's ear, "I'll be waiting for you."

The Snarlies immediately took off into the cloudy night sky and circled high above the robots. They came together in what could only be called *The Dance of The Gooba-Gum Snarlies*. Dancing like a pair of prima bikie ballerinas, and snorting up as much gooba as they could from their mucous membranes, Flip and Flop released a blanket of their gummiest gooba to snotdrop on the robots, and with the greatest of ease, it stopped the metallic monsters in their tracks.

The attack had been foiled and thanks to the Snarlies, Charlie and the animals could emerge from their hiding places. Now it was the turn of the cougars and the cheetahs. With one silent leap, their sinewy bodies flew over the walls of Weavel World and opened the gates for the animals and Charlie to enter.

Once they were inside, Charlie and his menagerie were confronted by real life safari rides and whiz-bang sideshow alleys where you could toy with any animal that tickled your fancy. Near to completion, these hideous diversions were ready to start making oodles of money for the evil Weavel when the park opened the following day. The animals gasped in distress when they saw their own kind stuffed and stuck to lamp-posts and billboards lining the streets.

Now Skunk Weavel pulled his master-stroke. From the top of a merry-go-round that was full of bounceless kangaroos the Toyminator appeared with a huge sledgehammer in his bony hands. He started to sing *Old Macdonald Had a Farm,* swinging the hammer against a large gong with each *ee-eye ee-eye oh.* The reverberating clanging sound brought to life all the lifeless animals. Ripping themselves down from their perches, they started moving threateningly towards Charlie and his comrades.

As if in a trance, Skunk's automatons inched nearer and nearer, forcing Charlie and the animals into a corner. They hissed and spat at their brothers and sisters who were in shock and distress in having to fight their kinsmen. Gradually, the spiritless creatures inched menacingly closer, determined to finish them off.

"Stop! Think of what you're doing! You're letting the Toyminator win!" the animals screamed at their brainwashed cousins. But their attempts to stave off the attack seemed futile until they heard a whistling sound from above. Thunder Eggs started dropping from the night skies like water balloons. The Eagle Air Force had returned. The eggs smashed against the ground directly between the two groups, releasing gallons and gallons of life restoring egg yolk.

"Tell them to eat the yolk! Show them the way! Eat the yolk!" shouted Charlie. The animals began scooping up the golden antidote to feed to their vacant brothers and sisters. As the magical elixir was devoured, the stuffed animals left the world of plush and cuddlydom and returned to the land of the living, reuniting with their brethren. The battle was over.

The search now began for Skunk Weavel.

After his rooftop appearance, Skunk disappeared, leaving them wondering where he could be within the vast park. Diving into corners and avoiding potholes, the teddy bears led the desperate search for the elusive madman and Penelope. The group was almost at the point of giving up when Sir Edward Bainbridge saw a light flickering from a fabricated building—an animal testing laboratory that was barricaded with boards, barbed wire, padlocks and chains. This was Skunk Weavel's new headquarters—his bunker.

"This way dear fwiends. This is where the wahscal has taken wehfuge. I can smell his malodowous odor," said Sir Edward, sniffing the air and adjusting his monocle. Very quickly, the Snarlies picked the locks to the concrete doors. Led by Listen-To-The-Wind, the animals were ready to enter the bunker when Charlie stopped them.

"Listen everyone, this is my responsibility. I have to rescue my sister and save *The Book*. Otherwise all is lost." There was a general murmur of uncertainty. The eagles wanted to capture the toymaker and fly him away to a place where he wouldn't cause any more mischief. The polar bears wanted to throw him onto an ice flow. The gorillas wanted to leave him in the mist of the forest, never to be seen again. But Charlie was adamant. Listen-To-The-Wind agreed to allow Charlie to enter the chamber and confront the toymaker. However, if there was any trouble, the eagles would be right behind him. And right behind them would be Flip followed by Snoozeball, a quivering Runningmouth whose claw was held by her dear Flop. Moon gripped Charlie's hand and whispered something in his ear. Charlie gulped, nodded, cleared his throat and pushed the door open. As he entered, all the animals snuck in behind him to watch the proceedings.

The chamber was lit by one fluorescent light, emitting only the barest illumination. In the weak light ahead, Charlie could see the pathetic paws of desperate caged creatures reaching out to be released. He weaved his way past numerous wooden crates filled to the brim with stuffed animals, all guarded by large sticky cobwebs that seemed to stretch out their fingers to try and entrap him. Very soon, he heard the familiar sound of Skunk Weavel talking—talking to *The Book!*

"The final page," hissed Skunk. "This is what must be printed, my treasure: *The evil animals and that rotten Ramsbottom kid all ganged up on the poor Skunk Weavelly-poo, but luckily, he managed to escape and live happily ever after in Weavel Wor-....*"

"Stop, Skunk!" shouted Charlie. "This is not finished yet," he said, emerging from behind a crate. Charlie stood, fiercely looking up at the toymaker. Skunk cradled *The Book* in his arms while sitting on a huge jeweled throne surrounded by undulating snakes and worms. Next to him was Penelope, gagged and bound to a chair, a jar of stuffing potion just inches from her.

"No, it's not finished is it?" spat the demented Skunk. The toymaker continued. *"Charlie Ramsbottom's legs started to give way under him."* Against his will, Charlie started to crumble. The brilliantly maniacal Toyminator was gaining control.

"Then Charlie Ramsbottom started to worship Skunk Weavel, his new master," screamed the toy-stuffing lunatic. Charlie knelt down and bowed to Skunk. Slithering snakes and worms crawled all over Charlie's face. Uncapping the jar of

potion, the toymaker screeched and howled with laughter.

"*...and on his hands and knees, Charlie Ramsbottom begged Skunk Weavel, Thy Great One,*" he continued, "*...to send him and his sister into the world of plush toys.*" Charlie repeated the words, his brain completely turned to spaghetti by the toymaker's diabolical rantings. Penelope tried to get out of her restraints but she was bound too tightly.

The slimy worms and slithering snakes pulled Charlie down into a position of even greater veneration of the all-powerful Skunk, who sat, eyes slitted, reveling in his new-found power. When Charlie finally hit the ground, the Great Conch of the Ocean fell out of his bag and onto the floor in front of him. Immediately, the conch was slimed by worms and snakes. Charlie had forgotten all about the shell but now, as his life rushed up before him, threatening him once more with a world of eternal cuddlydom and toy boxes, he saw a flicker of a chance. Realizing that he had one more blow of the conch, this being his second emergency, he grabbed the precious shell. Full of courage, he pulled off the worm-slime and the snakes, put it to his mouth and blew as hard as he could, even harder. But nothing happened. No sound emerged from the shiny shell; instead an amazing stillness filled the air, like the quiet that holds the sporting crowd as they anticipate the winning goal being scored in the dying seconds of the game. Without any warning, a loud whooshing sound erupted in Charlie's inner ear, there was an incredible flash of light and an eccentric looking man stood next to Charlie. He was wearing a heavy greatcoat and a pair of snow-colored gloves and tall black boots up to his knees. A most beautiful long white beard seemed to grow out of his face like a snowstorm of cottonwool and he had the deepest blue eyes Charlie had ever seen. It was Bizz-Buzz and he was carrying a giant flashlight.

"What do you want?" screamed Skunk contemptuously. Bizz-Buzz ignored his psychotic sibling and spoke with quiet assurance to an amazed Charlie. Taking off his gloves and shaking hands with our young hero, he said softly, "Hello Charlie, I'm Bizz-Buzz. Nice to finally meet you. Your journey is nearly completed, so stay true. Now is the time to restore the eagles to their rightful place. And the only way to stop Skunk is…" Bizz-Buzz stopped, leaned over and bizzed softly in Charlie's ear. Charlie stood up, looking concerned.

"But I don't know how to," said Charlie.

Bizz-Buzz responded with gentle authority. "Just trust that your heart will know what to do."

All the animals that had crept into the bunker silently rose from behind the boxes as Charlie faced the Toyminator.

"Don't believe him, Charlie," hissed Skunk. "He talks a load of claptrap." Bizz-Buzz gave Charlie an encouraging nod. Charlie thought to himself, stay true, stay true. He closed his eyes and just kept saying those words over and over again.

"Stuffed toy, you want to be a stuffed toy," hissed Weavel, trying to break Charlie's train of thought.

"Stay true—let the eagles fly again," said Charlie to himself.

"Stuffed toy…stuffed toy…"

"Stay true…fly eagles. Fly."

Skunk kept calling out but his voice seemed to fade, and Charlie felt like he was standing in a beam of white light. He was. Bizz-Buzz had turned on his giant flashlight and was shining it down on the boy. Charlie kept saying to himself, over and over again, "Fly. Fly eagles. Fly."

He then spread his arms and a magnificent pair of wings majestically burst from out of his pirate costume. He unfurled the wings and stood in front of the Toyminator.

"Listen to me, Skunk Weavel," he commanded, pulling off his eye patch. And without another word, he slowly started to sing a song that his parents often sang to each other. It drove Skunk absolutely bonkers.

Drea-ea-ea-ea-eam, dream, dream, dream
Drea-ea-ea-ea-eam, dream, dream, dream...

All the animals, led by Bizz-Buzz with his flashlight, stood side-by-side and joined in, swaying and waving their arms above their heads in unison.

Drea-ea-ea-ea-eam, dream, dream, dream
Drea-ea-ea-ea-eam, dream, dream, dream...

Instantly, the toymaker dropped the book, clamped his hands to his ears, rocked back and forth, and gnashed his teeth. At the same time, there was the hurried beating of tiny wings. Charlie looked up. It was Moon. The princely bird came flying through the room, and before Skunk realized what was happening, Moon had swept down and, with his beak, caught *The Book* just before it hit the ground. The victorious bird dropped the book neatly into Charlie's hands. Weavel squealed like a skunk and raised his leg to blast a Ferocious Attack of the Roaring Trumpets at everyone, but the Snarlies were onto him and pushed his leg down so that he blasted himself instead.

"Gotcha," cried Flip and Flop, holding their noses. "Animals are *us!*" they screeched proudly and nasally, high fiving each other.

"If there's one thing I can't stand in life Mr. Weavel, it's a bad sport," said Charlie, sticking his tongue out at him. With the Snarlies guarding Skunk, Charlie released Penelope, who looked at him sheepishly. She whispered, "Will you ever forgive me?"

"Only if you clean my room for a year," Charlie said jokingly. In profound relief, Penelope burst into tears and threw her arms around her brother.

All the animals cheered and clapped their claws. As the applause died down, Charlie opened *The Book* to re-read the part that Skunk had been reading when he first entered the bunker.

"The animals were saved by the egg yolk from the Thunder Eggs. Skunk Weavel managed to escape but they caught him at Weavel World where he made a promise that he would work with the dream-team to protect animals all over the world." Charlie stopped for a moment and smiled at Bizz-Buzz. Then he continued. *"Finally, the eagles' wings were restored and they took their rightful place in the skies and..."*

"Never, never, never! I'll never protect animals! They're useless, just like you lot," screamed a very hysterical Skunk. By now, he was surrounded by everyone urging him to be good.

Instead, he grabbed hold of the potion, raised it in a defiant toast and poured it slowly down his throat. Then he licked his lips and cackled.

Silence!

Those in the bunker took a collective deep breath as they watched Skunk Weavel turn into a stuffed and fluffy toymaker right in front of their very eyes. Charlie felt a little claw holding his hand. It was Moon. He whispered to Charlie, "Go on. You must finish from where you began. It's close to midnight and *The Book of Dreams* must be restored before the clock strikes twelve."

Charlie spoke slowly and confidently, "...and the doors for all dreamers were able to be safely opened again. And...they all lived happily ever after!"

Just as Charlie said his last word, the clock began to chime. It chimed twelve times. Everybody cheered. Charlie wanted to make sure that the adventure was complete, and moved closer to the frozen figure of Skunk. He looked deep into the toymaker's eyes. For a moment, he thought he saw a flicker of life in Skunk's malevolent gaze and could have sworn he heard a hiss emanate from the purple lips. But no, he was just imagining things, wasn't he?

As Charlie and the animals made their way outside to continue the celebrations, hundreds of children from the City of the Quincequonces who had gathered in anticipation, broke into spontaneous applause. While the ovation rang out, Sir Edward Bainbridge stepped forward to make a speech.

"Charlie Wamsbottom," he said. The crowds of children and animals fell silent.

"Sir Edward," said Charlie.

"Dear fwiend, call me Teddy," said Sir Edward.

"Teddy, please continue," said Charlie.

The monocled leader began his speech. "Fwom this day on...teddy bears will make it their wesponsibility to quietly live in toy shops all awound the world to make weally sure that no one like Skunk Weavel ever gets to wun a toy shop again." When Sir Edward finished, the animals parted to make way for Bizz-Buzz. On his arm was Doreen Tremblingknees. She was dancing.

"Charlie and Penelope. You've met my niece, Doreen." They welcomed Doreen while Bizz-Buzz placed *The Book* in between them on a table. He continued,

"Charlie, dreamers from all over the world will be grateful to you forever. You stayed true and as a sign of your connection to all those you have rescued, Thunder Egg Farm will now become a sanctuary to all creatures great and small. You have proven yourself to be a boy of substance, a boy who loves animals, and a boy who follows his heart. So from this day forward, you will be the protector of all Thunder Eggs and the endangered animals that seek safe haven on the farm. Now, please let us join hands."

Charlie, Penelope, Doreen and Bizz-Buzz held hands. Moon perched on Charlie's shoulder. And with the animals watching on in silence, Doreen broke into song, a beautiful song in which she was joined by Penelope who sang the most surprisingly wonderful harmony. And then, to everyone's delight, I-Can-See-For-Miles added her heavenly voice. The show was over and the fat eagle was finally singing. The song went like this:

The time has come for us to rejoice
The prophecy, a brave-hearted boy
Has put his trust in a spirit unknown
The gift has been given,
The seedling has grown.

Charlie suddenly felt an electric tingle run through his body. When he looked down at *The Book*, he saw the title of the jeweled cover change from *The Book of Skunk Weavel Rules* into its correct title—*The Book of Dreams*.

Bizz-Buzz stroked his wonderful snowy beard, winked at Charlie and picked up *The Book*. He was just about to speak again when Snoozeball and Runningmouth pushed their way to the front of the crowd and bowed to Charlie.

"Oh, great Egg-Master," said Snoozeball to Charlie in jest. "Two Thunder Egg Chickens have a simple request." Charlie was bemused.

"What is it, Snoozeball?" asked Charlie.

"Well actually, we would like permission to finish our game of Happy Families with Flip and Flop." Charlie laughed, nodded his head and then created his first edict: "Thunder Egg Chickens and Snarlies, go for it! Enjoy yourselves, but one word of advice; listen to Mr. Flop a little more as he has a much better understanding of the game than you think." Flip looked at Flop with a brand new respect and Flop looked like he'd won a million dollars. Runningmouth was extremely proud as she stood by her man.

The Thunder Egg Chickens and the Snarlies did a round of high fives and rushed off to play the hand of hands. As they did, one of the children in the crowd looked to the sky, pointing.

"What are those?" called the child, watching the dark clouds run away from the city, leaving the kidnapped moon free to illuminate the sky once more. There was a hush, and everyone looked up, amazed at seeing a beautiful, unpolluted starlit sky.

Listen-To-The-Wind answered the child, "Those are stars, my young friend. Stars. That's the Milky Way."

Listen-To-The-Wind turned to Charlie.

"Charlie Ramsbottom. You have saved us from a world of dark silence, one that I could never allow myself to imagine. I am in the twilight of my reign, and tomorrow as the sun rises, my son Prince Golden Moon will begin his training to become the next King of the Eagles. In gratitude for all that you have done for us, and as you possess true Eagle Spirit, we would like to give you the one thing that you would most wish for."

Charlie's first thought was of a brand new deluxe edition EM9.

"Think deeper, Charlie," Bizz-Buzz bizzed. "Think back to the dream."

Charlie closed his eyes for a moment, picturing himself in front of *The Book of Dreams,* Bizz-Buzz by his side. Suddenly, he remembered what he had been about to say when the Snarlies had interrupted his dream. Now he could complete his wish. Charlie took a deep breath and spoke, repeating the words exactly as he recalled them, "If I could have one wish, I'd wish I could...fly."

"So be it!" said the King and Bizz-Buzz together, grinning

at Charlie.

"Can Penelope come too?" asked Charlie. Penelope looked completely surprised and very pleased.

"As you wish," said Listen-To-The-Wind. He turned to his winged commanders and said, "Please carry Penelope above this world in your safest formation."

"What about me?" asked Charlie.

"You don't need us to help you, Charlie, you know that. You are Eagle Spirit."

Listen-To-The-Wind and the great eagles lifted off with Penelope above the masses of children and animals that cheered and clapped and whistled. Charlie flapped his wings and within seconds was airborne flying alongside Moon.

With Listen-To-The-Wind and I-Can See-For-Miles leading, the flock of eagles and Charlie rose rapidly into the air, circling and spiraling above the City of the Quincequonces. Drifting higher and higher on the thermal currents, they soared above the clouds. Through the misty cumulus, Bizz-Buzz appeared, his arms spread as he kept up with the eagles.

Bizz-Buzz held *The Book of Dreams* up high. A beautiful sparkling energy filled the air. Charlie felt as though his heart would burst. He looked across at Penelope, whose mouth was wide open in disbelief. It all seemed so unreal but incredibly real. And then Moon swooped across Charlie's flight path and flew alongside him. They looked at each other and flew wing to wing. Moon nestled into Charlie for one last moment, dipped his wings and banked away, calling out in a trembling voice, "I will never forget you!"

The band of eagles continued circling and spiraling, spiraling and circling. Suddenly, Charlie felt himself alone in the night sky as he soared higher and higher. It was the most exhilarating feeling. Then all at once, his world went into a spin and it seemed like someone was shaking him, calling him to get out of bed. Someone *was* shaking him! It was his sister.

"Happy birthday to you. Happy birthday to you," sang Penelope melodiously. "I hope you had lovely dreams."

"Kind of," said Charlie, rubbing the sleep from his eyes. "What day is it? Where am I? What's going on?" he asked, lifting his head. He looked around. The package! It was still there on the table, unopened. His schoolbag was on the floor where he had left it. Penelope started to leave the room.

"Wait, P." She turned at the door. He grabbed his skateboard from under his bed. "Do you want to ride Lucky to school today?" "Wicked, Cree- Charlie," she said smiling at him and rushed downstairs.

Charlie jumped out of bed and went to get dressed when he realized he was wearing pirate pajamas. Charlie looked back at his bed. It was full of feathers, eagle feathers.

Quickly, he rushed to the window. He tried to open it but it was double-locked. Releasing the stiffened bolts, he pushed the window open as hard as he could, and immediately a huge flock of birds flew by and seemed to stare at him. Charlie did a double take. Then he looked down at the tree where he'd held Moon in his arms and where the Snarlies had flown over them. A red double-decker bus, blaring South American music, passed on the road below the farm and the female ticket collector seemed to hang out from the door and wave to him.

Sylvia Ramsbottom called for him to come downstairs. He rubbed the sleep out of his eyes. It couldn't have all been a dream, could it? Leaving the room, something caught his attention, the calendar with the picture of the eagle on it. The eagle had a strong resemblance to Moon. Charlie picked up his gift, left the room and went downstairs shaking his head.

Reaching the kitchen, he could hear voices. Slowly, he opened the door. There on the breakfast table was an enormous birthday cake. It was shaped like a number nine. The room had streamers and party decorations all over it. Charlie's parents must have been up all night preparing. Seated beside Sylvia and Cecil at the table were Noni Benoni, Mr. Eric Grumblebum and Penelope, who gave him a big toothy smile.

"Happy Birthday, Charlie," they all said aloud. Charlie sat down and opened his gift. Inside the wrapping paper was a small book.

"Look Mum, look Dad! It's called *The Adventures of Charlie and Moon.*" Charlie's parents leaned over and looked at the book. On the front cover was a painting of Charlie flying through the sky with an eagle. When Charlie opened the book, a blue and gold winged eagle's feather dropped out.

"Shall I read it to you?" asked Charlie, his eyes sparkling as he held the feather.

"Wait a moment there," said his father, passing another gift to Charlie. Charlie opened the silver gift-wrapped box to reveal two tiny chocolates sitting there just waiting to be eaten. One was in the shape of a rose, the other, a conch. Charlie looked up and laughed. His parents laughed. Penelope laughed. So did Noni Benoni and Mr. Grumblebum.

Sylvia Ramsbottom poured the tea as Charlie picked up the two chocolates and looked at Penelope. She met his gaze.

"Do you remember when you shattered the eggs?" he asked quietly. Penelope replied with her own question.

"Wicked! Do you remember flying with the eagles?" Charlie smiled and nodded as he passed Penelope one of the chocolates.

"Ready then?" he said. She nodded. "One, two, three!" And they both popped the chocolates into their mouths at the same time. Charlie slowly opened his book. If he had looked up at the kitchen windows, he would have noticed a multitude of animals (all last seen at Weavel World) watching him while he prepared himself to read. And if he had looked further afield, he would have seen that the sign at the farm gate now read:

THUNDER EGG FARM ANIMAL SANCTUARY

An eccentric-looking man was striding along the path away from the farm acknowledging the multitude of animals that had come to bid him farewell. His sturdy black boots crunched against the stony terrain as he carried a gnarled, wooden walking stick. He was wearing a heavy greatcoat and a pair of snow-colored gloves and he beamed a huge smile at all those assembled. The man stopped for a moment and undid his greatcoat revealing a flash of his red suit as he pulled out an ancient seashell from an inner pocket. Putting it to his lips, he blew it like a didgeridoo. As the sound resonated across the valley, he looked up to the sky and the tinkling of sleigh-bells filled the air. Suddenly, a blizzard of snow erupted in front of him and he stepped into it, completely disappearing.

Turning to page one, Charlie started to read his story, *"It was an unusually warm night in the shire of Tumblegum..."*